Unspoken

The Unraveled Series

Book One

K A Fisher

First published by Unraveled Press, 2025

First edition

ISBN: 979-8-9990092-0-3

Table of Contents

<u>Content Warning</u>

This novel contains themes of sexual assault, trauma, pregnancy resulting from assault, and mental health struggles, including panic attacks. Reader discretion is advised.

While this story is fictional, it explores real emotional experiences with care. If these topics are sensitive for you, please proceed with caution.

Prologue

Some stories begin with clarity.

A single moment. A single choice.

Mine didn't.

It began with silence.

A space I don't remember entering.

A voice I nearly recognized.

A name that wasn't mine.

When I opened my eyes again, everything had changed.

For weeks, I tried to forget—

to bury it beneath deadlines, polite smiles, and unanswered calls.

But truth doesn't stay silent forever— not when it's stitched into your skin and rooted beneath your ribs.

This is the story of what I tried to escape—

and what caught up with me anyway.

But it's more than just my story.

There are parts I'll never be able to explain.

Moments I only saw from one angle.

Truths I never tried to understand.

A single voice can't hold the whole truth.

Others are waiting—

to finish what I couldn't.

This story doesn't end with me.

Chapter One

Eve sat on the edge of the bathtub, the pregnancy test trembling between her fingers.

Outside, the city shifted beneath a late September sky—twilight brushing the skyline in hues of rose and gold.

One word stared back in sharp digital letters:

PREGNANT.

Her throat tightened. The bathroom fan hummed steadily overhead, a low, thoughtless sound that tried to drown out what she wasn't ready to name.

She stayed still, breathing slow and shallow. Her hands barely shook. Her pulse, though, was pounding at her wrist.

Earlier that evening, she'd searched in half-hearted desperation: 'late period but not pregnant' 'can stress delay menstruation'

The headlines were enough to terrify her.

She hadn't wanted to know. But she'd hoped for mercy. For clarity.

Instead, there it was: the thing she couldn't unknow, the thing she hadn't dared to say aloud.

A knock at the door.

"You okay?" Maddie's voice came softly through the wood. "Want me to pick the movie?"

Eve shoved the test into the pocket of her old sweater and flushed the toilet.

"Yeah. Give me a minute."

She caught her reflection in the mirror. Pale. Lips pressed too tight. She splashed water on her face, watching it drip from her chin like rain. She looked composed. That was the lie.

The box and wrapper were already gone—tossed in a trash can outside the drugstore. Just in case Maddie ever went digging.

Back in her room, she hesitated. Then she buried the test in the nightstand, under loose tissues and tangled cords. Out of sight. Like it would buy her time or give her a choice.

Maddie had queued up a movie and poured two glasses of wine. The coffee table was a sprawl of snacks—popcorn, peanut M&M's, leftover Thai spring rolls. Their usual Sunday routine. Familiar. Comforting.

Eve folded onto the couch, limbs heavy and uncertain. Maddie handed her a glass.

"I think I'll skip tonight," Eve said, forcing a smile. "Stomach's a little off."

Maddie raised a brow. "You've been off all day. You barely ate."

"Nerves," she lied, grabbing a spring roll she didn't want. "Tomorrow's the big day."

Maddie softened. "You'll crush it. You always do."

Eve nodded, though her smile didn't hold. "Months of prep. I want it to be perfect."

She tugged a blanket over her lap, layering distance between them.

Maddie pressed play. Blue light flickered across the room. She laughed at a line they'd memorized years ago.

Eve didn't.

The silence that followed wasn't long.

"Seriously, what's going on?" Maddie asked, pausing the movie. "You've been... somewhere else lately."

Eve's pulse jumped.

"I'll be better after tomorrow," she said. Even. Practiced.

Another lie. One Maddie let slide—out of trust, or out of grace.

They finished the movie in silence. Not the comforting kind. The kind that makes every crack feel like a spotlight.

That night, Eve sat in bed with her laptop open, the screen casting shadows across the sheets. The blinking cursor felt too loud.

Work was usually her refuge—the one place she didn't have to perform.

She wasn't careless. She'd been cautious. In control.

But that night hadn't left room for caution.

She opened a browser tab and typed: 'Planned Parenthood near me'

Then deleted it.

She tried again: 'how soon do symptoms start...?'

Closed the laptop. The click startled her.

Eve curled inward.

Her phone buzzed once. Ignored.

Again. A calendar alert: *Ashcroft Strategy Sync – 10:00 a.m.*

She turned out the light.

Not from exhaustion. From weight.

Her father had chosen her to lead this project—one of Whitmore's most prestigious clients.

She'd show up.

No one would know. No one could suspect.

But tonight, she let herself crack—just a little.

Because it was the only way she knew how to keep the rest of her intact.

Chapter Two

Eve – Two Months Earlier | Charleston, South Carolina

I had dreamed of Charleston's thick air, tangled ivy, and saltwater clinging to every breath. The streets curled into hidden alleys, brick walls stained with age, shadows pooling like secrets waiting to be uncovered.

The flight was uneventful—hours of clouds and slow anticipation.

Late July heat pressed in the moment I stepped outside. I peeled off my cardigan, tucking it into my bag as sweat beaded at the base of my neck.

The cab ride into the French Quarter blurred past in snapshots: moss-draped oaks, shuttered windows, wrought-iron balconies, manicured courtyards.

The hotel was elegant and understated, tucked near Waterfront Park.

Inside, the lobby shimmered with soft music and low laughter. Guests lingered near the bar, champagne glasses catching the light. Something was being celebrated. A wedding, maybe. The woman at the front desk smiled as if welcoming me into a secret world.

The room was small but charming, with French doors that opened onto a narrow balcony. Below, the streets glowed gold beneath the heat.

I changed into a soft dress, dabbed on perfume—my usual blend of citrus and jasmine. Familiar. Grounding. Something to make me feel like myself.

Outside, I wandered without direction, drawn toward the water. Past hand-holding couples, tourists with cameras, a street musician playing blues beneath a flickering lamp.

Dinner was quiet—a salad and sparkling water at a café nestled beneath an ivy-covered awning. I sat by the window, watching the harbor darken.

I paid, but I didn't rush. The air was still warm, the light slipping into dusk. I walked toward the Pineapple Fountain, passing palms and fountains, the scent of magnolia and sea salt weaving through the air.

Then I saw him.

A figure stood just beyond a lamppost, hood up, face hidden by shadows. Hands in his pockets.

He stepped forward. Not fast. Deliberate.

Like he knew me.

A breeze stirred. Jasmine.

"There you are," he said, arms slipping gently around my waist. "I almost thought you wouldn't come."

My body went still. I didn't know him.

"I've been waiting... watching the clock... counting the minutes."

"I'm not—" The words broke.

A soft laugh. "You always do this... but you come back."

His breath touched my neck.

I tried to step away. He didn't notice.

"We only have tonight," he whispered, guiding me forward like it was muscle memory.

"I hate leaving... without you, it's not home."

My pulse raced. My limbs went numb.

He led me off the sidewalk, behind a hedge-lined garden.

"You said this was perfect. That nothing else mattered."

I froze.

His fingers traced my wrist. Meant to soothe. It made my skin crawl.

"You were shaking," he said. "Our first time."

"Please... you have the wrong—"

But he didn't hear me. Or couldn't.

His hands moved like he was remembering.

Not hurting. Just... wrong.

He spoke to someone who wasn't me.

"You said... I was yours."

I couldn't speak.

"You're mine," he whispered.

Every word separated me further from myself.

My body unhooked from my mind.

Time blurred.

I don't know how long I was gone.

When I came back, it was in fragments—like surfacing

from a nightmare I didn't remember entering.

My dress was twisted. Rumpled.

I never said yes.

Not to him.

Not to this.

A sliver of light pierced the hedges.

It hit just enough—to catch it.

The ink.

Faint. Blurred.

But the placement seared into memory.

I shoved him. Hard.

He stumbled, confusion in his voice.

"Sadie...?"

I ran.

The city melted into motion—light, sound, panic.

I didn't stop until I reached the hotel.

The doorman stepped aside without a word.

Inside, the celebration continued behind closed doors.

My hands trembled as I unlocked the room.

Only after the door clicked shut behind me did I

collapse.

Chapter Three

Everything I'd been holding together since the alley gave way the second I crossed the threshold.

The sobs hit fast—jagged, unrelenting.

The dress. The shoes. Soaked in him. Contaminated. Unwearable.

I ripped them off in frantic motions, dropping the pile near the door like it burned.

In the bathroom, I twisted the shower knobs until steam hissed through the air. The mirror fogged.

I stepped under the spray and scrubbed until my skin turned pink—everywhere he'd touched.

The jasmine clung like a ghost. His voice echoed beneath the water.

I collapsed to the floor of the tub, arms wrapped around my knees.

Eventually, the water turned cold. I climbed out, wrapped myself in a towel, and curled into the bed—a hollow shell of stillness, letting the last of the tears fall.

She didn't sleep.

Exhaustion pressed down, but every time her eyes fluttered shut, he returned. His breath. His voice. The weight of him. That flash of ink, seared into memory.

The panic came in waves, pulling her under. Moonlight spilled across the floor. The bathroom light glowed beneath the door.

She gripped the blanket tighter. Armor.

Then it hit: tomorrow, she was expected to pitch strategy. Shake hands. Smile.

Ashcroft.

It was the most important client she'd ever led.

And there was no way she could do it.

The thought gutted her.

Her father's voice echoed: *Ashcroft chose us because they trust us.* He'd called it *her* project. Her moment.

She'd spent months preparing. And now, she couldn't even breathe without breaking.

The phone glared from the nightstand: 3:41 a.m.

Blake.

She typed:

Eve: I'm so sorry to drop this on you. I'm unwell. Can you take the Ashcroft meeting? Everything's in the shared folder. I owe you—big time.

Minutes later:

Blake: Got it. I'll take the meeting. We'll catch up when you're back.

No questions. No judgment. Just Blake.

She opened her laptop, fingers trembling. Typed quickly, cleanly.

Subject: Scheduling Update

To: Natalie Hayes

Dear Natalie,

Apologies for the short notice—I'm unable to attend today's session due to unforeseen circumstances.

Blake Andrews will present on my behalf. He has all the materials and is fully briefed.

Thank you for your understanding. Best,

Eve Whitmore

She hovered. Then hit send.

One more message to go.

Her father.

But she couldn't do that yet. She set the phone aside.

That truth would have to wait.

The airline app showed an earlier flight. She booked it.

Canceling a meeting, rescheduling a flight—that she could do. Saying what happened? She couldn't even say it to herself.

She just needed to get home.

Outside, morning light crept across the balcony. She moved on instinct—packing in silence. She left the ruined clothes. Tossed the perfume. Zipped the suitcase.

Called for a cab.

Five minutes later, the hotel phone rang. The sound made her flinch.

She scribbled a note for housekeeping. Left a tip that was too much.

The elevator ride was slow. A man stepped in. His cologne—spiced leather and mint—was unfamiliar. Still, she held her breath until he got off.

The doorman opened the door with a kind smile. Outside, the city moved on—joggers, trucks, clattering heels.

She was invisible to all of it. A shadow moving through.

At the airport, everything overwhelmed her. Lights. Voices. Luggage wheels clicking.

She pressed her spine against a column, eyes down, fists clenched.

She pulled out her phone:

Eve: Picked something up. Stomach's a mess. Blake's covering. I'll fill you in when I'm back.

Sent it just before boarding. A buffer. An excuse. A way to avoid hearing his voice.

The flight passed in a blur. She didn't remember takeoff or landing.

When her phone buzzed, it was from her father:

Dad: Understood. We'll debrief soon.

It felt like a warning. And a promise.

The apartment was empty when she got in. No footsteps. No voices. Just silence.

And in it, she unraveled. Alone.

Chapter Four

Present Day | Hayes Valley, San Francisco

Monday arrived, and Eve had been up long before the alarm—well before the sun. That was the rhythm now: wake in the dark, outpace the dreams, and navigate the wreckage without drawing attention.

Maddie was already in the kitchen when Eve emerged—barefoot, a protein bar in one hand, her blazer slung over the other. "You've got this," Maddie said, handing her a coffee. "Ashcroft doesn't stand a chance."

Eve managed a smile. "Thanks."

Maddie gave her a once-over, eyes sharp but warm. "You've been laser-focused for weeks. They're lucky to have you."

Eve shrugged as she slipped into her blazer. It was snug across the ribs. She didn't let herself dwell on why.

"Let's hope they agree."

"Your pitch is flawless," Maddie replied with a grin.

Eve turned toward her room, protein bar in hand. She set it down on the bed and sat at her vanity. Reaching for her perfume, she stopped mid-motion.

A faint trace of jasmine hung in the air.

Her stomach twisted.

Charleston.

She dropped the bottle into the trash. The clink echoed—too final, too loud for the quiet.

By nine, she was in her office, finalizing the slide deck. Sunlight streamed through the windows—clear and warm, rare for late September in San Francisco. The fog had lifted, replaced by a breeze that smelled of salt and eucalyptus.

The office buzzed. Footsteps echoed down the hall. Laughter spilled from the design corner. Client calls drifted through open doors. A cart of mock-ups rolled past. Espresso scented the air.

The energy was electric—Ashcroft's meeting at the center, but a dozen other projects thrived too.

Eve tuned it all out. Her focus was narrowed to one slide, one morning, one pitch.

At 9:45 sharp, a knock. Her father stood in the doorway—Ellis Whitmore. "You ready?" he asked, voice light, pride flickering behind his eyes.

She stood. "Yes."

This moment had lived in his hopes for years. She still remembered trailing behind him as a child, asking questions he always answered like they mattered.

Now, it was real.

She knew the pitch—every slide, every strategy. She'd built it. But beneath it all, something fragile pulsed. What if I fall apart?

They walked together to the glass-walled conference room.

Two Ashcroft reps sat at the long table. One stood.

"Holden Ashcroft," he said, offering a steady hand. "My father sends his regrets. Something urgent came up back East."

She'd known Hayes Ashcroft wouldn't attend, but she hadn't expected his son. She thought the team would handle it.

Her pulse quickened at the shift in expectation.

She stepped forward and shook his hand. Warm. Grounded.

"Eve Whitmore. Thank you for coming."

He smiled. "Your firm came highly recommended—for honoring heritage while bringing fresh perspective. That's what we need."

He gestured to the table, voice calm and assured. "The floor is yours."

Her voice was clear: "We project a 15% increase in repeat guest bookings within six months if we launch the loyalty app alongside the rebrand."

Holden listened—fully. Not a flicker of distraction.

When he asked questions, they were sharp, strategic. She answered without hesitation.

By the end, her father nodded. Melissa Kane, the second Ashcroft rep, looked impressed.

As the group stood to break for lunch, Holden lingered. His eyes flicked to Eve, measured.

"Any good lunch spots nearby?"

She hesitated. A simple question. But simple things had grown complicated.

"Bianchi's," she said. "Casual but good."

He nodded. "Care to join me?"

There was no flirtation—just professionalism.

The invitation surprised her. Lunch had become another solitary routine. Safe. Predictable.

But this wasn't a date. It was business. Something her former self wouldn't have questioned.

She started to decline. Then her father stepped in. "Great idea. You've earned it."

She glanced at Holden. He said nothing—just smiled and pressed the elevator button, gesturing for her to step in first.

She did. A quiet boundary crossed.

Lunch at Bianchi's was disarmingly easy.

A small, familiar place—a few blocks from the office.

Always smelling of garlic and basil.

They sat by the window.

Eve didn't open the menu. "Margherita," she said.

Holden followed suit.

He didn't fill the space with small talk or overreach.

Professional—but not stiff. Measured. Present.

He asked about campaigns. She shared a college pitch

story she rarely told.

"Let me guess," he said. "QR codes on business cards?"

She winced. "Worse. Hashtag campaign for gluten-free

dog treats."

His laugh was low and real. When hers followed, it surprised her.

She hadn't laughed in months—not since Charleston.

The armor slipped. It felt reckless to enjoy it.

He noticed. She felt it in his gaze—softened, but not searching. Just attuned.

Still, she didn't retreat. And that shocked her.

Since July, she'd feared being seen—truly seen. She avoided attention, eye contact. Exposure.

But Holden didn't ask for more than she could give.

He carried something, too. She could sense it in his posture. The stillness in him. A careful weight.

It wasn't flirtation. It was recognition.

Two people carrying things they didn't speak of—still showing up.

Back at the office, paperwork circled the room. Pens clicked. Pages turned.

Ashcroft + Whitmore. Signed. Sealed. Real.

Eve stared at the page an extra beat. Months of effort—rescued from unraveling.

Her father beamed. Melissa Kane offered a firm handshake.

Holden said nothing. But when their eyes met, she saw it—respect.

She tucked the folder into her portfolio and stood. A long breath steadied her spine.

Holden waited near the lobby, coat folded over his arm.

"Could we exchange numbers?" he asked. "For coordination."

It was professional. Direct. Honest.

She handed him her phone.

He typed, then looked up. "You were formidable today."

The words landed. She hadn't realized how badly she needed them.

"Thank you," she said softly.

He nodded, turned, and walked toward the elevator.

Melissa waited.

Eve watched until the doors closed.

There'd been no flirtation. No warning bells—the kind she'd trusted since that night.

And that unsettled her.

Letting her guard down meant risk. Pain. Vulnerability. Abandonment.

And this time, she didn't know if she'd survive it.

She tried not to dwell. He was a client. Flying home soon.

Just another closed file. That's all it was supposed to be.

Chapter Five

The office was already humming when Eve arrived. Phones ringing. Laughter spilling from the kitchen. A typical Tuesday at Whitmore Consulting.

Outside her window, the morning light was sharp and clear—crisp for late September. San Francisco was wide awake.

She slipped into her office, set her coffee down, and opened her laptop with practiced precision. The motion was muscle memory now—an anchor in the swirl of everything else.

The night before, Maddie had greeted her with takeout and wide-armed celebration.

"You did it," she'd said, eyes shining.

But success didn't feel like a clean break from the fog.

Maddie expected her to move forward now. To

emerge.

Eve wasn't sure she could. But she knew she had to try.

Ashcroft + Whitmore was officially in motion.

The biggest account Eve had ever led—one shaped by

her from the inside out.

Congratulations trickled in: nods in the hallway, Slack

messages, and a company-wide email from her father.

Just one word: Proud.

He didn't use it casually.

It was nearly noon, and still—no triumph. No release.

Blake sat across from her, reviewing final branding

mockups: signage, keycards, digital check-in screens.

He tapped his pen against the Ashcroft folder. "This is good. Solid transitions. It's gonna land well."

"Thanks."

She reread the closing paragraph of the slide deck. No changes needed. Her hands were steady. Her voice was even.

Then the nausea crept in—sharp, uninvited.

She shifted, inhaled through her nose, reached for her water.

Not now.

She pulled open a drawer, grabbed the apple slices she'd packed that morning, and took a bite. The tartness grounded her.

Blake didn't notice—still flipping pages, unaware.

She glanced at him—and suddenly, memory flared.

Three days after Charleston, her father had called a debrief.

Just the three of them.

Eve had walked into the boardroom with her spine rigid and her excuses rehearsed.

Blake had already been there, laptop open, posture casual.

"Welcome back," he'd said, like it was nothing. "Hope you're feeling better."

"Stomach bug," she'd mumbled. "Hit hard."

Her father had raised a brow—but let it go.

They'd jumped into timelines, strategy shifts. Blake had taken the lead.

He gave her credit where it mattered, shielded her in ways no one else saw.

And when the meeting ended, he'd looked her squarely in the eye.

"You ready to lead this?"

She'd nodded.

"We've got this," he'd said.

She never forgot it.

Now, across from her, Blake flipped another page.

She turned back to her screen, but her mind had wandered.

Her fingers tightened around the apple.

A wave of knowing churned inside her.

The desk phone rang.

"Hello?"

A pause. Then: "Hey."

Warm. Low. Steady.

Holden.

Her pulse stayed even, but something inside her

exhaled.

"How are things on your end?" he asked.

Not for updates. Not to check a box.

Just... asking.

"Everything's lining up. No fires," she replied, eyes

drifting to the Ashcroft folder.

"You're thorough."

"I didn't say thank you yesterday," he added. "Not properly."

"You kind of did."

"But I meant it. More than I said."

A pause.

"My father doesn't hand out projects like this," he said. "He's selective. You earned this, Eve. Every bit of it."

The dread she'd carried all morning shifted—loosening, just slightly.

She didn't respond right away.

Across the room, Blake stood and gave her a wave. She returned it, half-aware.

She wanted to say something—but couldn't yet.

So she let the silence do the work.

It didn't hover awkwardly.

It settled.

"I fly out early tomorrow," Holden said. "Thought I'd grab one last dinner. Any local recommendations?"

The invitation was in the tone. Soft. Intentional.

Before she could answer, he added, "You could join. No pressure."

Her body went still.

Dinner. At night. In a space she couldn't control.

Brick. Jasmine. Wrists. Panic.

He must've felt the shift.

"Bring a friend," he offered, voice gentler. "If that helps."

She didn't say yes.

Didn't say no.

"I'll check in later," he said.

She set the phone down.

Reached for her cell.

Eve: Are you free tonight?

Maddie: Always. Why?

Eve: Dinner. It's tentative. I'll let you know.

Maddie: Whoa—social plans? Is this your grand return?

Eve: Don't make it weird.

Maddie: Too late. Already dressing emotionally for the occasion.

Eve: Maddie...

Maddie: I missed you. It's good to see this side again.

Eve smiled faintly.

The rest of the day blurred:

Client calls. A forgotten lunch. She completed Emails

and task lists on autopilot.

At 4:03 p.m., her phone buzzed.

Holden: Dinner. Mahogany. 7:00.

Her reply was quicker than expected.

Eve: We'll be there. I'm bringing my friend, Maddie

West.

The second she hit send, the weight of it landed.

What did I just agree to?

Buzz.

Holden: Meet you in the lobby.

She stared at the screen, then opened a new message.

Eve: Dinner. 7 p.m. Mahogany.

Maddie: Already picking earrings.

Typical.

One steady breath.

No turning back.

Back at the apartment, Eve stepped through the door.

Maddie looked up from the couch. "You don't text dinner plans without context. Spill."

Eve dropped her bag. "Holden Ashcroft."

Maddie blinked. "That Holden Ashcroft?"

"It's just business."

An hour later, their bedroom looked like a boutique exploded.

Dresses. Heels. Options.

"Black wrap dress," Maddie said. "The one that makes you look like you came to conquer."

"I was going to wear—"

"You're wearing the wrap dress."

Eve gave in.

"You're really leaning in."

"I haven't seen you leave the house for anything but groceries since July," Maddie replied. "I'm not missing your first night out."

Eve pulled the dress over her frame.

It fit differently now—tight at the ribs, stretched across her waist.

She felt the shift.

Knew what it meant.

She didn't let herself dwell.

Maddie reappeared in green, radiant. "You okay?"

"Yeah."

A practiced lie.

Maddie held her gaze, but didn't push.

"Then let's go."

Union Square shimmered.

The hotel lobby glowed—vaulted ceilings, warm brass,

jazz in the air.

Holden stood by the private elevator, relaxed in navy

and denim.

Next to him, a man with dark eyes and effortless charm.

"Eve," Holden said. "This is Jax Maxwell. Jax—Eve Whitmore. Maddie West."

"Nice to meet you," Maddie said.

"You too," Jax replied with a grin.

The elevator chimed.

They stepped inside.

Eve moved to the back.

Then—spice. Cologne. A memory.

Her fists clenched.

Panic rose fast, unannounced.

Then—Holden's hand. Gentle. At the small of her back.

Not pressing. Just present.

She didn't flinch.

She didn't move.

And that terrified her more than the panic ever had.

Mahogany's dining room glowed—glass and velvet, candlelight and linen.

A table near the window. Soft lighting. Familiar tension.

"Water, please," Eve said quickly as the sommelier approached.

Maddie's glance was brief—but perceptive.

Jax lightened the mood.

Holden told stories.

Eve listened. Present.

They ordered.

Holden chose the filet. Eve did too.

No commentary.

Just water passed her way. Quiet understanding.

The meal passed gently.

Laughter. Storytelling. Glimpses of ease.

Eve ate.

She smiled.

She didn't disappear.

In the lobby, the city pulsed through the glass.

Maddie and Jax exchanged numbers near the exit.

Eve lingered beside Holden.

"Thanks for inviting us," she said.

"I didn't think you'd come."

"I wasn't going to."

"Why did you?"

"I don't know."

He didn't press.

"Goodnight, Everly," he said.

She hadn't told him that name.

But it didn't feel wrong.

"Goodnight, Holden."

She stepped into the night.

Didn't look back.

Because somehow—without meaning to—

He'd reminded her what forward felt like.

Chapter Six

The Ashcroft deal had wrapped. Mahogany was behind her. But three weeks later, its weight still lingered.

Outside, autumn had settled in. The air held a drier chill now, edged with the scent of tarweed. Leaves scraped across the sidewalk like secrets trying to be heard.

Eve stared down at her planner, a thick line drawn beneath Monday: Charleston. The ink had bled slightly, smudging beneath her fingertip.

It felt inevitable.

Charleston wasn't her choice. Even the name scraped like grit across her nerves.

She hadn't planned to return. Whitmore's long-tail team usually handled final rollouts—but her father had insisted. Said she needed to be visible. Present. That it was important to close out a client of this size in person.

He didn't know what he was asking. And she couldn't say no without raising a red flag.

So here she was. Carrying her signature strategy all the way to the finish line, pretending it didn't cost her anything to show up.

Blake had already confirmed hotel blocks. The obsessive pace kept her upright—task to task, minute to minute, mechanically precise.

Her days were full: conference calls, client meetings, finalized documents.

The occasional text from Holden came—efficient, intentional, brief. Still, they lingered longer than she wanted them to.

He hadn't been part of the project before San Francisco. Until that meeting, she hadn't even known his name. She hadn't expected to work with him again.

He wasn't supposed to be at the San Francisco meeting. And she hadn't planned to go to Charleston.

Now, they'd meet again.

She wondered why he'd stayed involved. He hadn't been up until the pitch. Maybe his father needed him. Maybe he'd been behind the scenes all along.

She didn't ask. She told herself it didn't matter.

But the part of her that had started to breathe again in San Francisco wasn't so sure.

No matter how deeply she buried herself in spreadsheets and strategy, the memories still found cracks to slip through.

Grocery store lines. The scent of jasmine. A certain streetlamp glow.

It took almost nothing to send her spiraling back.

She hadn't chosen a path—not out of indifference, but because choosing meant naming things. Losing the comfort of not knowing.

But she'd started thinking.

Late at night, alone in her room, the silence made space for questions she wasn't ready to answer.

She searched aimlessly. Tabs opened in private browsers and closed just as fast—Planned Parenthood. Pregnancy resource centers. Adoption agencies.

Each one felt foreign. Like a road she couldn't follow.

Sometimes she imagined keeping the baby. Other times, placing it with someone else.

And once—just once—she lingered on a page titled *Your Options After a Positive Test*, wondering what it would mean to end it.

She never got far with that thought.

Her hand often pressed lightly to her stomach—just a subtle shift in her center of gravity, as if her body knew before she did.

The nausea had dulled, but her body was changing. Quiet signals she didn't yet know how to interpret.

Long hours left her exhausted, off-balance, aware of a presence she hadn't acknowledged aloud.

Nothing obvious yet. But the truth wouldn't stay hidden much longer.

The weight of secrecy pressed in like a vice.

She wondered if the decision would be easier if she talked to Maddie. Or her parents. If she said the words aloud.

But the fear was louder.

Maddie didn't question. She knew Eve's rhythms. When she withdrew, it meant she was deep in something. Trying to control the outcome. Pushing never helped. So she didn't.

They stuck to their routines—morning coffee, Friday takeout, weekend errands. Small things that anchored them.

Jax had become part of that rhythm, too.

One night, she came home to the smell of basil and roasted tomatoes curling through the apartment. Maddie stood barefoot at the stove, stirring sauce while Jax chopped herbs beside her.

"This is not a real knife," he complained, holding up the dull blade like it had betrayed him.

Maddie laughed—loud, full, unguarded. "It's a paring knife, Gordon Ramsay."

"It's a war crime," he said, but he smiled as he passed her the basil.

They moved easily around each other. The kind of closeness built without effort.

Some days, it soothed her. Other days, it reminded her how misaligned she'd become.

From her desk, Eve looked up.

"Did you talk to your mom yet?" Maddie asked.

"Not yet."

"She'll call again."

"I know."

She closed her laptop. "I'll call her back today."

"She's worried," Maddie said, gentler now.

She wasn't wrong.

The worry began the day Eve returned from Charleston. She'd missed the biggest meeting of her career with a vague stomach bug excuse. Her mom didn't push—at first. She showed up a day later with broth and too many questions.

Eve had barely held it together.

She remembered it clearly: her mom standing in the doorway, concern etched into every line of her face, arms half-lifted like she wasn't sure whether to reach for her or not.

That look—the aching tenderness—nearly undid her.

She couldn't tell her. Couldn't explain what had happened. Or how the fear still lived inside her.

So she'd smiled weakly and said she was tired. Blamed sushi. Walked her to the door and promised to rest.

A lie dressed in responsibility.

Since then, she'd kept her distance—short replies, timed check-ins, polished excuses.

Her mom kept trying—voicemails, texts, a few unexpected drop-ins at the office. Not out of impatience, but love.

Eve was her only child. And distance had never sat well with her.

But lately, it wasn't working.

Her mom wasn't letting go.

And Eve...

She wasn't sure how much longer she could hold the line.

Her emotions felt like a hairline fracture—one more tap and everything might break open.

There were close calls.

Leaving her laptop open with a browser tab she forgot to close.

Reaching for ginger tea in the grocery store, only to hear Maddie tease, "What are you, seventy?"

Placing a hand over her stomach and realizing Maddie had seen.

The dinner invitation came after a stretch of avoidance. Saturday night. Her childhood home.

Eve had said yes before she could think.

Another excuse would have drawn more attention than just showing up and pretending.

But the idea of walking through that door—seeing her mom, wondering what they might notice—that rattled her.

She could manage clients. Could command a room.

But her mom? That was different.

She wasn't sure she had the strength to fake it again.

She already knew what would greet her: Rosemary from the kitchen. The trace of her dad's cologne. The lemon-slick polish on the stair rail.

That night, she lay in bed, eyes on the ceiling as the city hummed through the window.

Her hand rested lightly on her abdomen.

She was still building her courage.

Some days, she felt strong enough to keep going.

Other days, the smallest thing might undo her.

Her phone lit up: Holden's name.

She turned it face down.

Unread.

Sometimes silence felt safer.

When she finally opened it, the message was strictly

professional:

Holden Ashcroft: Everything still good for Monday?

Let me know if you want someone from our team to

meet you at the airport.

Nothing more than logistics.

But it landed with weight.

She reread it. Then again.

It lingered like an open door—waiting. Patient.

For a version of herself she wasn't sure she knew.

Not yet.

Maybe never.

Chapter Seven

Maddie climbed the long hill into Pacific Heights, where autumn had settled in full.

The drive felt different—lighter somehow, but laced with expectation.

There was something about Saturday evenings. The city didn't stop, but it changed. The frantic energy of the workweek gave way to couples strolling hand-in-hand, dogs tugging at leashes, and laughter rising from sidewalk patios.

"You okay over there, or are you mentally rearranging the pantry again?" Maddie asked, glancing sideways, her voice wry beneath the low hum of jazz.

Eve blinked, caught. "What?"

Maddie smirked, but it didn't hide the worry in her eyes. "You've been staring out the window like you're alphabetizing the spice rack."

Eve managed a soft laugh. "Just thinking."

Maddie didn't press. But the silence that followed wasn't casual.

Eve had promised she'd feel better after the Ashcroft deal closed. That the fog would lift. But the contract had only extended. And for Eve, it became the perfect excuse to keep hiding.

But something was looming.

She'd grown quieter over the past week—more precise. Like every thought had to pass through a filter before being spoken.

She was sealing the cracks.

The edges of her composure frayed—just slightly.

Enough to make her afraid of what might spill through

if she stopped pretending.

A dull ache had settled into Eve's lower back,

persistent now.

"You sure you don't want me to pretend I forgot about

this dinner?"

"No. If I skip it, she'll call every day for a week. Might

as well go in person."

Maddie didn't argue.

They turned onto a tree-lined block, frozen in time.

Every house wore its autumn uniform—symmetrical

pumpkins, clipped hedges, wreaths hung with surgical

precision. The Whitmore house was Victorian, with

dark green trim, tall windows, and the same sprawling oak that once dropped acorns on cool autumn days but now dropped memories without warning.

The porch light glowed. A harvest wreath hung from the door—twigs, burnt orange leaves, sage sprigs, a velvet ribbon tied just so.

"She went full catalog," Maddie muttered.

"She always does."

Eve stepped out of the car and drew in a breath. The scent of damp earth and sea salt hung in the air, anchoring her to the moment.

The door opened before they could knock.

Her mom, Claire Whitmore, stood framed in warm foyer light, glass of wine in hand. Slate blue cashmere, pearl studs, hair swept back with practiced elegance. She wore poise like perfume.

"Girls," she said, brisk but warm. "Come in—it's been too long."

"Hi, Mom." Eve managed a faint smile.

"Thanks for having us," Maddie said, sliding into charm mode.

Inside, the house looked like a fall lifestyle spread—cinnamon candles flickering, soft music on the stereo, decorative gourds clustered on the entry table. It was her mother's signature—rituals timed to the calendar like clockwork.

She closed the door behind them. "Your father's in the kitchen, perfecting the potatoes. You know how he gets."

The scent—rosemary, garlic, a hint of cracked pepper—hit Eve immediately. It was comforting. A recipe he'd mastered during her college years, always saving it for the weekends she came home. That smell had meant safety.

Eve nodded and unbuttoned her coat. Her mom's eyes scanned her with practiced precision. Not suspicion— just that soft, maternal scrutiny that always saw too much.

"Big week?" she asked, taking their coats.

"The rollout meetings start Monday. We fly to Charleston in the morning."

She lifted a brow. "Already?"

"We're ahead of schedule," Eve said, tucking her hands into her pockets. "It's the final phase."

"She's been on calls in her sleep," Maddie added, smiling. "I think the hotel staff in Charleston knows her voice better than her coworkers do."

Her eyes glanced back at Eve. "Just don't forget to take care of yourself while you're charming the Ashcroft team."

"I'll be fine," Eve said, voice practiced. She had said it so often, it almost sounded true.

Her dad appeared in the doorway, beaming. "There's my strategist."

"Hi, Dad."

He pulled her into a hug. "Well, look who's out of the office."

"Briefly," she said, a small smile forming.

He nodded, reaching for the salt. "Nice to see you

without a laptop."

"Don't get used to it."

"Wasn't planning to. But it's good."

He turned to Maddie, grinning. "You keeping this one in line?"

"She's all business," Maddie teased. "I'm just here to lighten the mood."

"Good. We need that."

The dining room was immaculate—crystal glasses, linen napkins, polished silver, a low centerpiece of dried florals and cinnamon sticks in a copper tray.

They sat. Eve took her usual spot—central, but never close enough to draw focus. Maddie complimented the plating and the sea bass.

Eve pushed food around her plate. The fish unsettled her, so she stuck with potatoes and greens. Each bite was deliberate. Controlled.

She lifted the bottle. "Wine?"

"Early flight," Eve said, shaking her head. "Water's fine."

Her mom nodded, topping her glass with a slow, deliberate pour. "Of course."

Her gaze fixed a moment too long, but Eve didn't flinch. Across the table, her dad and Maddie had fallen into an easy conversation about traffic on the bridge.

Then Maddie glanced over. "She's been buried in work—her calendar since July makes mine look like a nap schedule."

She smiled, distracted just enough. "Well, tonight we slow it all down."

Eve gave her a quick look of gratitude. Maddie couldn't know—but she deflected like a pro.

Conversation drifted to safer ground—Blake's press mention, her mom's latest committee, a neighbor's failed kitchen renovation.

Eve contributed when prompted. She talked about rollout timelines, stakeholder dinners, and Ashcroft's historic property tour.

But her mom circled back.

"You've been working nonstop," she observed. "You look pale. Worn down."

"I've given this everything I have," Eve said, steady but thin. "Once it's done, I'll come up for air."

Her mom's silence wasn't empty. Eve recognized the quiet filing system behind her eyes—cataloging, comparing, storing what didn't add up.

Her mom always noticed more than she let on.

After dinner, they moved to the sitting room for dessert. The pear tart radiated warmth. Jazz hummed beneath the candlelight.

When it was time to go, she handed them their coats. Her hand paused on Eve's arm.

"You've never been as unreadable as you think, sweetheart," she said, voice soft. "But I'll wait until you're ready."

Eve's spine stiffened.

Her mom kissed her cheek. "Drive safe."

Outside, Maddie looped her arm through Eve's.

"She didn't say it outright, but..." Eve trailed. "She knows something's off."

Maddie shrugged. "You've got Charleston next week, a major launch, a million things on your plate—you're allowed to be a little off."

Eve didn't respond. Her gaze lingered on the porch one last time.

The porch light glowed—a steady, familiar beacon. It had once meant home.

Now, it belonged to a version of her she wasn't sure she could return to.

Chapter Eight

Eve navigated the apartment as if its very foundations might crack beneath her. Every step was carefully calibrated, every breath a conscious effort. One wrong move, one second too long in the mirror—and the illusion she'd barely held together all night would shatter.

Her mom's words echoed in her skull, dull and relentless: *You're not as unreadable as you think.*

That wasn't maternal intuition. It was a warning shot. The mask was slipping, and Eve knew it.

Only the kitchen light remained on, casting a soft glow across the otherwise dim apartment. Maddie's door was now closed, the thin sliver of light from earlier extinguished. Unaware of the storm brewing down the hall.

Eve crossed the living room, her bag and scarf lay untouched, right where she left them.

She stood at the window, pressing her fingertips to her temple.

The headache had started sometime between the second course and dessert. Too many unanswered questions behind her mom's careful gaze. Comments that landed with precision—about her complexion, her energy, the way she picked at her food.

She'd survived it. Barely. But at what cost? She felt the closeness she once had with them slipping further out of reach.

The exhaustion wasn't just work—it ran deeper, threaded through every part of her. She'd read enough to know the signs: first-trimester fatigue, nausea, food aversions, the unpredictable swell of emotion. Twelve, maybe thirteen weeks along by her estimate. Her body was changing in incremental, relentless ways. And layered over it all—stress, secrecy, trauma—she felt herself stretching thin, close to breaking.

In her room, she paused at the nightstand. A framed photo sat atop it—her and Maddie at graduation. Sunlight in their eyes, arms linked together, their futures wide open. That version of herself felt miles away.

She opened the drawer.

The folded tissue caught her eye. She didn't move it, just stared for a second too long. Beneath it, the test waited. Unchanged. Untouched. But very much present.

She pushed it farther back, more out of instinct than intention. She should have thrown it away. Keeping it wasn't simply careless; it was a tether to a truth she wasn't ready to face but couldn't quite let go of either.

Her suitcase sat ready in the corner—packed, zipped. Everything was in its place—neat, measured. Except her.

She wasn't ready.

Eve sank onto the edge of the bed. The desolation of the apartment pressed in. Still hiding.
Still alone.

Her window was narrowing.

And she knew—after Charleston, she'd have to stop pretending. She'd have to tell them. Maddie. Her parents.

Make a choice.

But she couldn't do it without a plan. That wasn't how she operated. But this was something far messier. The uncertainty terrified her, but the denial wouldn't save her anymore.

The terminal at SFO buzzed with early motion—rolling suitcases thumping against polished tile, the hiss of espresso machines, the low hum of gate announcements layered over it all.

Eve spotted Blake at Gate 26, leaning one elbow against the counter, nursing a cup of coffee as he chatted with the gate agent. The slight bounce of his heel gave him away—he was energized.

He turned as she approached, with a teasing grin. "Morning. You look ready."

"Generous of you." Her brow furrowed as she adjusted the scarf around her neck.

Blake lifted his cup slightly. "Coffee?"

She shook her head. "I'm good."

He nodded, taking another sip. That was part of what made working with Blake bearable—his steady professionalism and his ability to read a room without letting on.

Over the past few months, they had spent more time together than either of them planned—late nights, client calls, and strategy sessions that turned into genuine friendship.

Blake joined Whitmore shortly after she did. Her father introduced them on his first day. They clicked fast—both drawn to historic spaces, both detail-obsessed.

The Ashcroft rollout became their passion project. Not just a job. A shared vision.

And now... it was here—implementation week.

After this, they'd move on—assigned to different accounts, separate teams, separate paths.

She hadn't said thank you, not for Charleston. It sat inside her chest, unspoken—like a letter she couldn't quite send.

Their flight was delayed due to a mechanical issue.

By the time they found their seats, her team's energy had dwindled. The window offered only a glimpse of the overcast sky, which made the whole day feel like it was on pause.

Eve's shoulders were tight. Every part of her felt slightly out of alignment.

Blake settled beside her, flipping through the in-flight magazine without really reading it.

"You haven't said much," he said as the planc taxied.

"Reviewing the rollout steps."

He glanced at her. "You've been doing that for two weeks."

She gave him a faint smile. "It helps."

They both knew the strategy was airtight. Every touchpoint scripted, every stakeholder accounted for.

It was all second nature now.

But it wasn't the plan she was rehearsing; it was the act of holding herself together through it.

Somewhere over Nevada, the hum of the engines melted into white noise. Eve drifted—half-asleep, half-calculating.

The logistics made sense. The messaging was tight. But the rest? Remained uncertain.

She hovered in a strange in-between—a version of who she'd been and the woman she hadn't yet become.

They landed after dark.

The day had been a logistical mess—delays, gate changes, enough rebooking to drain any enthusiasm.

No one mentioned sightseeing after the third airline update. Chaos had handled it for her.

Holden's message still sat in her inbox:

Holden Ashcroft: Everything still good for Monday? Let me know if you want someone from our team to meet you at the airport.

She reread it—not for clarity, but for something unsaid. Some thread of familiarity. Safety. Or danger. She couldn't tell which.

A sliver of anticipation pulsed beneath her ribs.

She was going to see him again. Would it be the same?

The city sparkled beneath low haze, rain clinging to windows, wipers tracing slow arcs through the historic district. The roads looked the same, but each corner stirred something buried. Brick. A shadow. The wrong voice in the dark.

She kept her gaze locked on the window. Her palm pressed to her thigh. *Keep breathing.*

La Couronne de Laurier glowed ahead—arched windows framed by wrought-iron, golden lanterns glowing against stone. It rose like a secret behind hedge and wall, elegant and stoic. A flagship Ashcroft property. Now, her temporary home.

The cobblestones, slick with rain, blurred under the car's headlights.
Charleston didn't welcome her.
It watched—quiet, unblinking.

She stepped into the lobby, letting the smell of wood and bergamot calm her pulse.

It was stunning. A study in restraint and opulence. She could tell. She always could.

Blake handled check-in while she lingered behind, taking in the space.

Their rooms were on separate floors—a small mercy.

Inside her suite, relief came—not sharp or sudden, but slow, like her lungs had been waiting all day for permission.

The room welcomed her in muted tones—a tall, airy space with high ceilings and an oversized chair by the window. A tray of fruit and bottled water waited on the desk.

It was beautiful.

She didn't realize how much she needed beauty.

She unpacked—blazer hung, toiletries aligned, scarf folded.

She sat in the plush, oversized chair, picking up her phone again. Holden's message blinked on her screen.

She hovered a thumb above it.

Tomorrow...

What was in store for her?

Three months in, still secrets, still pretending. *You're not as unreadable as you think,* her mom had said. And she was right.

After Charleston, she would tell them.

She didn't know how the words would come—only that they had to.

No more drifting. No more hiding behind what-ifs.

Because this wasn't just her story anymore.

95

Chapter Nine

Pale, diffused morning light filled the hotel suite. Eve surrendered to the hush, lingering far longer than planned.

Outside, the breeze carried salt and woodsmoke. Late October had settled in—cool and dry, no longer clinging like July's heavy air.

Her appetite, for once, was steady—no knots, no nausea. Even her hair had thickened, catching the light with a sheen that startled her in the mirror.

This trip carved out space. A quiet pause between who she had been and who she might become. When it ended, she'd start the conversations.

She owed them that. But more than that, she owed herself the chance to begin again.

Adoption was the one possibility that didn't splinter her—yet. Could she look into a child's eyes and not search for pieces of herself—or him? She wasn't sure. But pretending it didn't matter was its own kind of lie.

She moved through her routine with care. This morning, it wasn't just habit—it was armor. A way to steady herself for the day ahead. For the version of herself she wasn't yet sure she believed in.

She studied her reflection a beat longer. Then slipped on her blazer, smoothed the sleeves, and stepped out to join her team for breakfast.

The buffet stretched beneath copper pendant lights— flaky pastries dusted with sugar, cast-iron skillets of rosemary potatoes, and chilled trays of citrus catching the morning sun.

Her stomach growled—a welcome surprise.

In the ballroom, the energy shifted as lights dimmed and the opening presentation began.

Ashcroft Management: 150 Years of Hospitality and History.

Sepia-toned images flickered—Charleston in the 1870s, slate rooftops, a modest inn by the harbor. A narrator's reverent voice carried them through wars, storms, and eras of reconstruction. The Ashcroft family had endured.

From guesthouse to legacy.

Near the back, she spotted him—Holden. Silent. Still. Watching her, not the screen.

The slideshow turned—preservation grants,
expansions, historic renovations.

Then—a photo. A formal garden estate. Twin boys in
pale suits.

No caption. No names.

But she knew what she was seeing. And more
importantly, what was missing.

She'd read every Ashcroft bio, every press release. Not
one mention. Not a line. It wasn't oversight. It was
erasure.

And that stirred something closer to recognition than
curiosity.

The morning unfolded—panels, sessions, property
updates. By noon, the buzz shifted toward lunch and a
historic walking tour.

Eve slipped out a rear ballroom door. The hallway offered a reprieve. Her fingertips brushed gilded trim, as if it might steady her.

Beauty lingered everywhere—restored tile, crown molding, amber light cast from old gas fixtures. Elegance, curated with reverence.

She considered disappearing for the afternoon.

Rounding a corner, she collided with someone.

Holden.

Beside him stood a poised couple—Hayes and Eliza Ashcroft. Their photographs didn't do them justice. Legacy softened by real edges.

Holden's face shifted when he saw her—something like relief. "Eve," he said. "Perfect timing."

He gestured toward them. "These are my parents—

Hayes and Eliza."

Eve stepped forward. "It's such a pleasure. The hotel is

stunning. Every detail feels intentional."

Eliza's smile bloomed, pride easing across her face.

"This project means a great deal to our family. I didn't

oversee the design directly, but—" she placed a hand

over her chest, "—it has my heart."

Hayes gave a nod, crisp and sincere. "I've followed

Whitmore's work. Not many impress me so quickly.

You've blended our legacy with something fresh—it

shows."

Warmth spread through her. "It's been an honor. The

bones of this building practically speak."

Hayes gave a low hum of approval. "My father used to say buildings remember who loved them."

They lingered a moment, discussing history. An 18th-century counting house had once stood beneath the hotel. During renovations, brick archways and iron hitching rings were uncovered—lost anchors brought back to light.

Eliza described the discovery like a keepsake. Holden added details easily, like someone raised in the story.

And for a breath, Eve forgot the weight in her chest.

A voice rang from the lobby: "All historic tour groups, please gather near the entrance!"

Hayes adjusted his cufflinks. "Looks like the adventure's starting."

Eliza touched Eve's arm. "We'll see you again before the week's end."

They moved off.

Holden remained.

"I'll walk you to the lobby," he offered.

They moved together, quiet. Around them, guides passed out name tags and clustered guests near the doors.

Eve hovered at the edge, breath caught somewhere between throat and ribs.

Her body wouldn't move.

Out there, the city was too exposed. Too familiar.

Her throat tightened.

Holden didn't press. He raised a hand—not to pull, not

to lead. A gesture. Simple. Still.

"No maps. No group. Just me."

The simplicity of it steadied her.

She glanced at his hand. Then his face. Steady.

Her legs still resisted.

But there was no perfect moment.

She gave a small nod.

Together, they stepped through the side door.

Holden didn't recite facts. He wove stories—

foundations saved one brick at a time. Forgotten

gardens restored. His grandfather's refusal to sell a

corner inn because it stood atop a carriage house.

They wandered a narrow alleyway. Ivy spilled from rooftops. Warm air curled around them like a memory.

He spoke of rooftop trespasses as a kid. His sisters. The summer they flooded a hallway mid-renovation.

She laughed. And for a while, her body forgot its burden.

Until they turned a corner.

Near the French Quarter, the street narrowed—brick underfoot, ivy closing in.

A café emerged.

Green and white awning.

Just like before.

Her heartbeat kicked up. Panic surged.

The city dissolved.

Brick. A voice. The dark.

Holden turned, smiling—then stopped.

"Eve?"

She blinked.

Tried to speak.

Nothing.

The sidewalk tilted.

Her knees gave.

The last thing she saw was Holden's hand reaching, shaky.

His voice sliced through the haze—urgent but far.

Then—

Silence.

No pain.

No sound.

Just his hand.

Still reaching.

Chapter Ten

Cold.

Then pain—sharp, clawing.

The world returned in fragments. Soundless. Slow.

She blinked once. Twice.

Shapes formed—a chair. A figure.

Then him.

Holden sat beside her. His jacket draped over the back of the chair, forgotten. Sleeves pushed past his elbows. Shoulders hunched. Head lowered. Hands braced between his knees like he was holding himself together by sheer will alone.

Her voice cracked. "Holden...?"

He stood instantly. "You're awake."

Something etched his face—relief, guilt, disbelief.

"You—God, Eve." He exhaled, hard. Ran a hand through his hair. "You passed out. On the sidewalk. You hit hard. I caught you, but... Jesus."

She tried to sit up. Pain flared along her spine. "Where am I?"

"MUSC. The ambulance brought you." His voice was steady. His eyes weren't.

It came back in pieces—curved brick, filtered light, ivy on a narrow street. Then sirens. The antiseptic sting of the ER. The jolt of gurney wheels. Ceiling lights flashing overhead. Beeping monitors slicing through the haze.

Embarrassment hit harder than the pain.

She had broken—and nothing about it had been graceful.

The curtain slid open.

A doctor entered, clipboard in hand, voice warm and practiced. "Miss Whitmore. You experienced a panic event—likely triggered by extreme stress and dehydration." He nodded politely toward Holden.

"We ran a full panel. No signs of concussion or cardiac concern. You're stable and cleared for discharge." He flipped a page. "The baby's heartbeat looked strong." A pause. "I'd suggest following up with your OB soon."

Everything inside her recoiled. Panic. Shame. Grief.

Her secret—spoken aloud. Unraveled by clinical phrasing and fluorescent lights. Exposed without permission.

The doctor looked up, eyes flicking between them. He cleared his throat. "A nurse will bring your discharge paperwork shortly."

Then he turned and left, the curtain swinging gently behind him.

Holden didn't speak. The air thickened between them—humming with a truth neither of them had intended to share.

He lowered himself into the chair like the truth might break him too.

"You're pregnant," he said finally, the words landing cold and real.

She turned away, voice barely audible. "You weren't supposed to know."

Her fingers gripped the hospital blanket like it might anchor her. Heat stung behind her eyes.

He stayed still, but she saw it—the slight drop of his shoulders, the line between his brows pulling together. Not in recoil. In something else.

Something she didn't expect.

His voice softened. "I told the nurse I was your partner."

She blinked at him.

"It was the only way they'd let me through." He dropped his gaze. "I didn't want you to wake up alone. But I crossed a line."

"No." Her voice caught. "You didn't."

She hadn't planned for him to find out. He wasn't supposed to be part of this story.

Holden rubbed the back of his neck. "I figured you were... guarded." A pause. "But I didn't know how much you'd been carrying."

Her breath hitched. "Please go," she said—too broken to be strong.

If she could be the one to end it, maybe it would hurt less than watching him choose to leave.

"I mean it," she added, louder now. "Just—go."

Still, he didn't move.

"I'm not—" Her voice fractured. "I'm not someone you're responsible for."

She braced for it. The retreat. The confirmation that her worst fears were true.

Because every time she'd imagined telling the truth, they walked away—disgusted, disappointed, done.

But then—quietly, steadily:

"I know that."

She swallowed hard. Her pulse thudded in her throat.

He leaned forward. His voice didn't shake.

"I'm not leaving."

Three words.

No hesitation.

And something inside her cracked—not from hurt, but from the shock of being chosen, right at the moment she least believed she could be.

She studied him. And for the first time, let herself believe that someone might know the truth—and stay.

The curtain pulled back.

A nurse stepped in—warm eyes, practiced hands. "Let's get you signed out, sweetheart." She wrapped the blood pressure cuff around Eve's arm. "Vitals look good."

She turned to Holden. "Can you pull the car around, sugar?"

He nodded, lingering a beat longer than necessary. "I'll see you outside."

The nurse patted his arm. "You did good, hon."

Once he was gone, she helped Eve into her shoes, removed the monitor leads, and explained the discharge papers. Her gentle presence felt like borrowed calm.

Eve nodded through it all, the storm still spinning inside her.

She didn't know what came next—but something had shifted.

Outside, the sun had begun to dip, setting the sky ablaze with fiery streaks. The temperature had dropped. Autumn was setting in.

The nurse wheeled her to the curb just as Holden's car pulled in. He stepped out, eyes locked on hers, and rounded to open the door without a word.

She stood slowly, testing her balance. Her body protested every movement.

"I can go back to the hotel—" she began, tentative.

He was already shaking his head.

"You're coming with me."

It wasn't a demand. Just a decision already made.

She stepped toward the car.

The leather was cool beneath her, cradling. The door shut with a soft, final sound.

Charleston faded behind them as they pulled away.

The Ashley River Bridge rose ahead—less a road than a threshold.

And in the low thrum of the drive, she clung to one thing:

She hadn't fallen.

She'd been caught.

And she didn't know what scared her more—the fall...

or the kindness that followed.

Chapter Eleven

The road stretched ahead in slow, winding curves, and with every mile, the city's rhythm fell away behind them.

Trees closed in around the narrowing path. Gravel crackled beneath the tires like a soft warning. It felt like crossing into another world.

At the end of the lane, a small cottage waited—tucked beneath an old oak, porch lights glowing amber across the path.

A retreat. Quiet. Steady. It asked nothing, offered everything.

Holden stepped out and came to her side. Eve hesitated, her hand hovering near the door. A dull ache pulsed through her hip where she'd landed, and the scraped skin on her knee flared as she shifted.

He offered his hand—not a demand, an invitation.

She slipped hers into his.

His touch lingered at her back as they climbed the steps. Each movement reminded her of how her legs had buckled, how the world had tilted.

At the top, he opened the door. "You first."

She paused. Then stepped inside.

The air smelled faintly of cedar. Soft light filtered through the space, rounding out its edges with quiet grace.

Muted blues, warm grays, and well-worn hardwoods greeted her. Built-in shelves held weathered books, scattered mementos, and photographs not curated for guests, but preserved for memory.

It was personal without feeling performed. A space shaped by someone who noticed, not someone who needed to prove it.

She paused at a photo—Holden, years younger, arms around two little girls in matching pajamas. In the foreground, two identical boys grinned, faces lit with Christmas morning wonder.

Joy hummed in the image. Honest. Unfiltered.

"I'll get you something to drink," he called from the kitchen. "Or food?"

She followed the sound of his voice, moving carefully.

The kitchen was compact but warm—marble counters, mugs hanging from hooks, spices lined up like a quiet ritual. A faint trace of clove and citrus hung in the air.

He stood at the sink, a glass in his hand. He looked composed, but she sensed the effort behind it.

"I'm sorry," she said, voice low. "I didn't mean to... break like that."

He crossed to her and tucked a strand of hair behind her ear.

"You didn't," he said softly. "You're carrying something that could undo anyone. And you've been doing it alone."

He stepped back, offering space. "I'll draw you a bath. Leave something clean to wear?"

She nodded. "That would be... nice."

He disappeared down the hall. She traced her fingers along the island's edge.

Her secret hadn't come from her mouth, but it had spilled all the same.

And still, he stayed.

"Eve?" His voice called gently.

She followed.

The bathroom was airy and quiet. The tub steamed, bubbles piled like soft clouds. A folded T-shirt and knit shorts rested on the vanity.

Lavender. Eucalyptus. A faint mineral warmth.

"Towels are in the basket. Take your time."

"Thank you."

Her shoulders dropped. A twinge flared in her lower back as she stepped forward.

He gave a nod and closed the door behind him.

She waited until his footsteps faded, then undressed slowly and stepped into the bath. The water welcomed her, warm and forgiving.

What if she didn't have to carry it alone?

Not love. Not rescue.

Just the choice to let someone in—on her terms.

Only when the water cooled and her fingers pruned did she stir.

A knock.

"You still in there?" Holden's voice, light. "Just making sure you didn't climb out the window."

A smile tugged at her lips. "Still here."

"Good."

She dried off with care, wincing at dull reminders, then slipped into the soft clothes he'd left.

When she returned, he was curled on the couch beneath a dim lamp—barefoot, in sweats and a worn T-shirt. He looked tired. Real.

She held out the clothes. He took them wordlessly. "I'll toss these in the wash."

"Thanks," she murmured.

She sank into the couch. A plate of fruit and bottled water waited on the table. Small comforts she hadn't realized she needed.

Holden returned, sitting beside her—close, but not crowding.

She looked over. "Why tell them you were my partner?"

He ran a hand through his hair, eyes fixed on the floor. "It wasn't planned. They wouldn't let me through. I panicked." He glanced at her. "I couldn't let you wake up alone. Not like that."

His words hit something unguarded.

He rubbed his temples. "Hospitals... aren't easy for me."

She didn't push. She respected what he wasn't ready to say.

"Today scared me," he added, voice quieter.

She turned toward him, her chest tight.

"I thought I had it under control," she said.

"I noticed." He gave a half-smile. "The way someone carries something too heavy for words."

She looked down. "I didn't think anyone could tell."

He reached over—slow, deliberate—and rested his hand near hers.

"It's late," she whispered. "I'll take the couch."

"I want you to take the bed," he said. "My room."

She shook her head. "Holden—really, I'm fine."

He didn't argue. Just gave a gentle, unwavering look. "Please."

She didn't fight him.

He led her down the hall and turned on the lamp.

The bedroom matched the rest of the house—simple, intentional. Navy duvet, crisp white sheets, no clutter. Just peace.

She slipped under the covers. The cotton cool against her skin.

He lingered just long enough to make sure she was settled.

"Will you stay?" she asked softly. "Just until I fall asleep."

He didn't hesitate.

He crossed to the bed and lay beside her—close, but not too close. His arm draped gently around her waist. His hand rested, warm and steady, against her side.

She didn't pull away.

Her body leaned into his—not out of longing, but recognition.

And for the first time, she let herself be held.

Chapter Twelve

A weight pressed against her chest—light at first, then suffocating. Not a dream.

Memory.

It clawed through sleep, dredging up what she hadn't invited.

The pressure deepened. Her body twisted beneath it. Sheets tangled around her legs. She thrashed.

She couldn't breathe.

Eve jolted upright, heart racing, a gasp tearing from her throat. Sweat slicked her spine. Her hip and back throbbed with each movement.

Her eyes darted.

Unfamiliar walls. Shifting shadows.

A voice pierced the haze—low, careful.

"Everly."

The name wrapped around her like a forgotten echo.

He didn't know that name. But somehow... he'd said it

like he did.

A soft click—the lamp glowed gold across the room,

softening the sharp corners of night.

Holden sat beside her, sleep-rumpled and still. Tousled

hair. Worn T-shirt. Shoulders hunched in concern. His

eyes met hers, steady.

He didn't reach for her.

He just watched—present, ready.

"It's okay," he said, his voice hushed. "You're safe here."

It was his weight, still beside her. His warmth.

She'd only asked him to stay until she drifted off. But

he hadn't left.

Her body trembled.

He shifted gently, reaching across her waist.

"Lie back down," he whispered.

His arm wrapped around her, steady and careful,

shielding her from the world.

The lamp clicked off.

Darkness returned, save the moonlight slanting

through the window—silver and soft across the sheets.

He pulled her close. Her back met his chest. His arm

curved around her like an anchor.

Tears came without warning.

Her voice cracked in the dark.

"Someone assaulted me."

No preamble. No buildup. Just truth. Raw and unflinching.

Holden inhaled sharply. His body stiffened behind her—only for a moment.

But he didn't move.

Didn't pull away.

Didn't let go.

The tears came harder now. She didn't fight them. She turned toward him.

He followed, his hand lifting to brush a tear from her cheek. His touch was warm. Unshaken.

"I haven't told anyone," she whispered.

She searched his face.

No pity. No distance.

Only grief.

And something sharper, coiled just beneath his skin.

Rage—but not at her.

At the world that had let it happen.

Then came the kiss.

Slow. Steady.

Not desire—something deeper. A vow to stay.

And in that kiss, something broke open.

She let herself shatter.

Tears surged in waves. Her body gave in, worn from

holding the weight alone.

He held her through it. Jaw tight, brow furrowed, as if

absorbing every ounce of her pain.

He didn't try to fix it.

"No one should carry that alone," he murmured.

The words weren't said with certainty.

They were said from experience.

He didn't ask for names.

Or how. Or when.

He just stayed.

His arms never loosened until her breathing slowed.

Until her sobs faded into silence.

Until sleep finally claimed her.

Relief didn't come all at once.

But it had begun.

And for the first time, she wasn't facing the storm alone.

Morning spilled into the room, golden and soft.

Birdsong floated in from the trees. Wind rustled the branches. Light pooled across the hardwood.

Eve blinked.

Her body remembered.

The weight was gone—but not the ache. Her side still throbbed. Her throat stung from tears she'd let fall at last.

She sat up slowly, back against the headboard.

No undoing it now. No retreating into pretense. Her truth had been spoken.

And he hadn't run.

The room came into focus—simple, curated, lived-in.

A jacket on a hook. A watch beside cufflinks. Books stacked neatly, dog-eared and worn.

Then she saw it.

Her luggage. Her work bag. Placed carefully in the corner near the bench.

Her breath caught.

A small gesture. Unasked for. Done with care.

She crossed the hall, drawn by the scent of garlic and butter.

Holden stood at the stove—barefoot, tousled, gray sweats slung low, shirt wrinkled from sleep. Light framed him like something cinematic.

He looked over. "You're up."

She nodded.

"Hungry?"

On cue, her stomach growled.

He chuckled. "I'll take that as a yes."

An omelet slid across the counter. A glass of juice followed.

She took a bite, then paused. "God. I didn't realize how hungry I was."

A beat.

"What time is it?"

"Ten-thirty."

Her eyes widened. "I had walkthroughs—meetings—I was supposed to—"

"Handled," he said. Calm. Unbothered. "I moved everything. We're working from here today."

"You did that?" she asked.

He shrugged. "You're not the only one who knows how to manage a calendar."

Her heart clenched in the quiet. "Thank you."

He nodded once, already sipping his coffee, returning to his laptop.

No questions.

No pressure.

Just space.

In the bathroom, she moved slowly—savoring the quiet. The window cracked open. Fresh air drifted in, threaded with the murmur of the river. Birds. Leaves. Real peace.

Her phone buzzed.

Maddie:

Hey, would it be okay if I borrowed your silver hoops tonight? Jax made dinner reservations. I want to look nice.

Eve:

Of course. They're in my room. Have fun.

She smiled. Real and small.

Maddie had found something bright again. Uncomplicated joy.

Eve dressed. The fabric of her dress clung a bit more than before—but she didn't try to hide. Not here.

She padded into the living room. Holden was already absorbed in emails, coffee beside him, sleeves rolled.

She moved to the couch with her laptop.

Eased into the cushions.

Still sore. Still healing.

Then—

She saw it.

Ink.

Clean-lined. Geometric.

Just below his wrist.

Her breath caught.

Not the design.

The placement.

Her heart lurched. Stomach flipped. Her vision narrowed.

A flash—skin, weight, a voice in the dark.

She clutched the arm of the couch. Tried to breathe.

She could forget the shape.

But not the location.

Never the location.

Holden noticed. Concern flickered.

"Stupid teenage decision," he said, trying for lightness.

"Snuck away on a beach trip with a friend. Thought we

were cool."

She nodded.

But didn't hear him.

Her gaze locked on the ink.

Same spot. Same place.

Her fingers twitched.

Coincidence.

It had to be.

She opened her laptop, hands trembling just enough to feel it.

Locked it away. For now.

Work had always been her disguise.

Not a lie—but an escape.

She loved it, honestly. But lately, it had become armor.

She clung to it now. Refining timelines. Reviewing projections. Lost in structure and numbers.

Holden mirrored her rhythm—parallel focus, shared silence.

They didn't speak much.

By dusk, Holden closed his laptop and leaned back.

"Enough?"

She nodded, shoulders stiff.

"Dinner out or in?"

"In."

He offered a stack of menus. She waved them off.

"Dealer's choice."

"Chinese," he said, already dialing.

They ate cross-legged on the floor, takeout containers scattered around them.

The fire crackled. Her pulse finally eased.

Later, she wandered to the bookshelf. Her fingers brushed familiar spines, paused near a frame.

A Christmas morning. Torn paper. Two little girls in pajamas.

And—

Two boys. Identical. Grinning wide.

He joined her quietly.

"My mom made us wait every year for the 'perfect shot.' We were animals by then."

She smiled faintly.

"Your sisters?"

"Bella and Ivy." His smile softened. "Bella's been to five continents. Ivy's a sophomore—she'd probably fight a bear if you gave her a reason."

Her gaze lingered.

"And him?"

He tensed.

"My twin. Levi."

A pause. The air shifted.

"We used to swap places. Got away with it all the time."

He laughed—soft, tired.

No stories after that.

No mention of now.

He set the frame back down with care, like it might break.

"Come on," he said.

The bedroom was cool and quiet. Cotton sheets. A navy duvet.

She slipped beneath them. He lingered at the doorway.

"Will you stay?"

A beat.

He crossed the room and lay beside her. Not close.

Just steady.

His arm moved around her waist.

She didn't pull away.

She leaned into him—not out of need.

But recognition.

And for the first time, she lived a day not built on

secrecy.

Not shaped by shame.

Just... lived.

Chapter Thirteen

Morning unfurled, spilling light across wide plank floors and into the corners of Holden's home. Shadows danced across shelves lined with worn books, polished frames, and objects he had chosen, not styled.

Eve padded into the kitchen, the scent of coffee trailing behind her. The hush of the house held, broken only by birdsong from the river. It was peaceful—the kind of morning San Francisco never gave her.

Inside, a quiet unburdening stirred—interrupted by the shuffle of clothes and the click of a buckle.

Tonight was the culmination of months of work. A celebration. Colleagues, clients, stakeholders. The final event.

Holden moved behind her, placing his phone on the dresser harder than necessary. His jacket was folded, his tie draped with care. He looked composed, but the ease was gone.

The phone buzzed again.

His jaw flexed. He checked the screen. "Give me a second." Not unkind—just clipped.

He stepped into the hallway and closed the door behind him.

She didn't try to listen. But his voice carried—low, tense, edged. When the call ended, the silence felt heavier than before.

She packed with care. Folding each item as if neatness might settle the unease tightening in her chest. Her side still ached when she bent.

Her flight was tomorrow. And with it—more hiding.
More waiting. Still no conversation with Maddie. Still
no word to her parents.

Holden returned, unreadable. Whatever the call
stirred, it hadn't passed. He didn't try to mask it.
Maybe he couldn't.

At the door, he paused—tie and keys in hand.

The signal was clear. It was time to leave.

She wasn't ready. But she nodded.

Instrumental music played low in the car. Charleston
drifted by—wrought-iron balconies, weathered brick,
gas lanterns burning softly in the morning haze. The
city felt suspended. Like it, too, was holding its breath.

The Ashcroft headquarters stood stately in South of
Broad. Whitewashed brick. Manicured hedges.

Wrought iron threaded with ivy. Every line spoke of legacy.

Inside, the scent of gardenias met aged wood. Archways carved by hand framed the entrance. The lobby buzzed—conference rooms full of movement, wall displays shifting, signage hung mid-adjustment, ideas becoming reality.

Holden nodded once and veered toward his office.

Eve pressed forward.

Blake was already in the conference room, coffee steaming beside his laptop.

Eve slipped into a chair and opened hers, fingers flying across the keys.

"Walk me through the guest suite updates. Did the signage changes make it into the final draft?"

Blake didn't answer right away.

"You disappeared yesterday," he said, glancing over.

Her shoulders didn't flinch. "Stress caught up to me," she replied evenly.

Her eyes stayed fixed on the screen—but her mind lingered in the hallway, in the silence Holden had worn like armor.

Blake studied her a moment longer. Not accusatory. Just... perceptive.

"I'm fine," she added, without looking up.

He didn't push. Instead, he turned his screen toward her. "Mockups came through last night. Suite Nine's lighting looks better now. Want to see?"

She leaned in.

And just like that, the rhythm returned. Project briefs. Vendor lists. Last-minute decisions. The structure wrapped around her like armor. Focus dulled the ache.

She was back in her element.

The rest of the day passed in blur—calls, confirmations, final walkthroughs. Precision was her mask. Control, her defense.

Holden remained distant. He was in and out of his office, always on the phone, face tight. If their paths crossed, it was brief—just a nod, just a glance.

Once, she saw him tucked inside a side office with Hayes. The door slightly ajar. Their posture mirrored— brows furrowed, faces drawn. Then, quietly, the door clicked shut.

He hadn't put the weight down.

By late afternoon, the team filtered back to the hotel to prepare. Eve lingered in the Ashcroft lobby, fingers trailing along the polished wood trim. She let her eyes close.

"Ready?"

Holden's voice cut through—smooth but subdued.

She turned. He stood near the door, coat in one hand, tie slung over the other arm. His face was neutral, but his posture had shifted. Shoulders lower. Eyes softer.

She nodded. "Yeah."

The drive to West Ashley passed in quiet. Dusk crept in, layering the trees in blue-gray shadow.

At the house, they dressed separately.

Eve stood in the mirror, pulling a black halter dress over her frame. It offered structure and grace without drawing attention—something she hadn't realized she needed. Her hair pinned in soft waves. Simple heels. She didn't aim to dazzle—just to feel like herself.

She opened her phone.

Eve: Landing around 6 tomorrow. Can't wait to see you.

No reply.

Strange. But Maddie was probably caught up in one of Jax's rabbit-hole stories, eyes glowing, laughter uncontrollable.

She tucked the phone away.

Probably just busy.

In the hallway, Holden crouched at the door, tying his shoes. When he looked up, he stilled.

Something in him eased.

"You look beautiful."

She let it settle. "Thanks. You clean up pretty well too."

She stepped closer, reaching for his tie. Her fingers brushed his collar. He didn't move.

The knot tightened beneath her touch. So did something between them.

And then—they stepped outside.

The air was crisp. The sky, brushed in amber. The city waited ahead.

***

The ballroom shimmered.

Lights draped from rafters. Chandeliers cast golden reflections. Tables glowed with glassware and linens.

Holden's hand found the small of her back—familiar now, but still grounding.

His parents stood near the center—Eliza luminous in navy silk, Hayes poised in slate gray. They drew focus without effort.

As Holden guided her toward them, the hum of conversation softened.

Hayes was first—warm, confident. He clasped Eve's hand in both of his.

"Miss Whitmore," he said, voice even and sure. "You've done exceptional work. What you've created honors our legacy."

Eve smiled, caught by his sincerity. "Thank you. Your hotels... they're remarkable. You've preserved what matters."

Eliza stepped closer, her hand brushing Eve's arm.

"You're bringing something rare," she said. "Modern grace without compromise. It's refreshing."

There was formality. But also mutual admiration.

Eve turned to Hayes again. "I also wanted to say—I'm sorry for missing our meeting in July. It wasn't planned. I hope your assistant passed along my message."

Holden stilled beside her. Just barely. She felt it.

When she glanced at him, his face gave nothing away— but his breath had paused.

Hayes waved it off. "Life rarely listens to our calendars. I missed San Francisco myself. Blake stepped in admirably."

He nodded toward Holden. "From what I hear, you've both done well."

Holden smiled. Slight. Hollow.

Eliza picked up the thread. "You've managed to honor history without being trapped by it. That's rare."

She touched Holden's arm—light, playful.

"You remember the Converse?" he asked, the corner of his mouth lifting. "She wore them to a board dinner. Swore they were vintage."

"They *were* vintage," Eliza said, swatting his shoulder.

The tension cracked.

Eve smiled. "Thank you. I should check in with the team before dinner."

Hayes nodded. Eliza's parting look lingered—a silent thread of pride.

At the bar, Blake leaned on the counter, glass in hand.

"You clean up well," she said.

He grinned. "So do you."

She stood beside him, letting the moment breathe.

"Thank you. For everything."

He raised his glass. "You did the heavy lifting."

She shook her head. "You carried more than you had to. We built something good here."

"Yeah," he said softly. "We did."

They stood in the hush of completion.

Then Blake's gaze shifted across the room.

"He keeps looking at you."

She turned. Holden—mid-conversation, hands in pockets. But his eyes were on her.

She looked away. "It's nothing."

Blake didn't press. "If it becomes something, no one would be surprised."

Before she could respond, Holden arrived.

"May I steal her for a dance?"

Blake stepped back. "She's all yours."

The chandeliers glowed above them.

Holden extended a hand. She took it.

They moved to the floor. Music swelled—slow, aching, rich with longing.

His hand found her waist. Her fingers rested on his shoulder. They moved as if they'd done this a thousand times.

Then—something shifted.

The music turned haunting.

She felt it, not in memory, but marrow.

The ache. The pull. The impossible longing to be seen—and unseen.

Holden said something—soft, meant for her.

She didn't hear it.

The melody clawed at her.

The walls pressed in.

"I'm sorry," she whispered. Her hand slipped from his.

She turned.

And disappeared into the crowd.

Holden didn't follow.

He stood still. One hand lowered, the other empty.

Watching her vanish into shadows and strings.

Chapter Fourteen

The air struck sharp—crisp, rich with the scent of dried leaves and damp earth.

Eve paced the sidewalk outside the hotel, her thoughts spiraling faster than her steps.

The string quartet's notes clung like cobwebs—delicate, inescapable.

What was she doing?

Or worse—what was she allowing?

A risk without a net. The past lay in wait, ready to swallow whatever fragile hope dared to form.

She wrapped her arms across her chest. The thin dress offered no protection from the chill.

She didn't hear him approach—

Not until his hand rose to her cheek, fingertips

brushing beneath her eye.

His palm settled there. Anchoring her.

"Everly."

She paused. Lifted her gaze, unsure what she'd find

looking back.

"I'm sorry," her voice cracked. "I—I don't know what's

happening. It's like everything's crashing at once."

Tears welled. She held them back.

"I want to go home," she whispered.

She hadn't meant her apartment. Or San Francisco.

She meant somewhere safer. Somewhere her body

didn't have to brace against the world.

Holden reached for his phone and called for the car.

Then slipped off his coat and draped it around her

shoulders—like a shield.

Letting herself lean into him—allowing him to carry part of what she couldn't name—was more than permission.

It was surrender.

They waited.

A suspended stillness they both understood.

The drive to West Ashley unraveled something in her.

Behind them, the city receded. Ahead, only sanctuary.

Crossing the bridge, she felt it. This was the in-between—not who she was, not yet who she'd become. She rested her head against the seat, watching shadows bend along the guardrails.

The fuzziness brought comfort. But the ache hadn't vanished.

It had simply altered.

From panic to possibility.

From drowning to choosing.

That's what Charleston had taken from her—not just safety, but choice.

And now, it was hers to reclaim.

The cottage appeared, dusky light glowing against the darkness, as if it had been waiting.

As the car stopped, Holden stepped out first.

She followed, still cloaked in his coat, the hem catching in the breeze.

At the porch, she hesitated.

One step back, and she vanished into the girl who kept hiding.

One step forward, and she chose to be seen.

She looked at the door.

Then at him.

And took the step.

Inside, the air was soft and weightless. She could finally breathe.

A room that opened up around her like an invitation to stay.

Eve stood just past the threshold, wrapped in his coat.

This stillness felt different. Not absence, but presence.

Holden hadn't moved.

He offered what she hadn't known how to ask for:

room to decide.

Her hands dropped. Her breath steadied.

For months, she'd lived behind a wall built from fear.

Tonight, she was choosing to step out from behind it.

She turned.

Each movement was hers—unhurried, intentional.

She slipped off his coat and draped it over the back of

the chair. Her fingers slowly fell away.

Holden hadn't moved.

His dress shirt was buttoned, tie loosened.

His posture said: *I'm here.*

No pressure. Just freedom.

She crossed the room, each step a deliberate

reclaiming.

When she reached him, she examined every feature

the way she did with spaces steeped in history.

Then leaned in and kissed him.

A declaration.

She moved to his buttons—undoing each one slowly.

With each pop of fabric, his breath shifted. His jaw

tensed. His lips parted, as if holding back words. Or

awe.

By the third button, his gaze dropped, watching her

hands.

His chest rose fuller. His throat worked to swallow

something unsaid.

He understood—she had to lead.

And that understanding became its own form of trust.

When the final button slipped loose, his eyes returned to hers—wide, glassy with something raw and reverent.

He reached up, took off his tie, and then his shirt fell to the floor with a soft sigh.

She pressed her palms to his skin.

Heat. Strength beneath the muscle. The steady thrum of his heartbeat—and the faintest tremble.

She closed her eyes. Let herself memorize it.

Her kiss came again—delicate, searing.

This time, he responded.

His arms wrapped around her. Not pulling.

As if to say: *I've got you, if you want to be held.*

She lifted her face. Their eyes met.

A moment passed.

Then she turned.

Her hands swept her hair aside, exposing her neck.

A silent signal.

He stepped forward.

His fingers brushed the nape of her neck.

Found the zipper.

Eased it down—slowly, honoring.

The dress slipped from her shoulders.

Pooled at her feet.

She stepped free of it.

Turned to face him.

A fragile hush unfolded between them.

No armor.

No hiding.

The soft curve of her belly caught the light.

His eyes found it—and held.

He stepped forward, as if something in him was drawn

to her—not out of duty, but something deeper. Quiet.

Unspoken.

Her hand moved instinctively to cover it—

But his rose first.

Not to stop her.

To ask.

No claim. Only recognition.

His palm settled over the swell, slow and steady. A

gesture of reverence, not possession.

She watched him.

Then placed her hand over his.

The silence pulsed with meaning.

She drew a breath, shallow at first. Then steadier.

"I haven't let anyone see me... not really..." she said, her voice trembling but clear. "Until now."

Holden looked up.

Something shifted behind his eyes—grief, understanding, and something like awe. A soft kind of knowing.

He didn't rush to fill the space.

Instead, he nodded once. A solemn promise tucked inside the gesture.

"I know what it means," he said quietly. "To let yourself be seen again. It's not small."

His hand stayed.

So did hers.

And when their eyes met, she didn't flinch or fold or retreat into the quiet she'd lived inside for so long.

She stood—unshielded, unhidden—because this time, she *chose* to be seen.

And for the first time in months, she didn't feel alone in it.

Chapter Fifteen

The first hints of dawn bled through the bedroom window—indigo and violet. The world felt suspended between night and morning.

"Everly," Holden said softly from the edge of the bed, his hand brushing her shoulder.

She blinked, still wrapped in blankets, clinging to the fragile tether of the night before.

She didn't want to move—but she did. Carefully gathering her clothes, she slipped into the guest bathroom.

Traces of the night lingered—his tie on the foyer table, her dress in a soft heap on the floor, his jacket draped over a chair. The house didn't just remember—it carried the imprint of something changed.

Holden offered to make breakfast.

She gave a tired smile and reached for an apple instead.

The drive to the airport was quiet, awash in the fading edge of autumn.

The seat beneath her was cool against her legs, the leather stiff from the morning chill. Music played low, saying something neither of them could.

Outside her window, Charleston stirred. Wrought-iron balconies, early light, the skyline shrinking with each passing mile.

His home had been more than shelter. It had been the one place she hadn't felt the need to hide—not from him, not from herself.

When he pulled up to the departure curb, he didn't shift into park right away.

"I should kidnap you," he said, a crooked smile brushing his mouth.

She smirked. "You'd look great in a mugshot."

Their banter was light, easy. Which somehow made leaving harder.

He stepped out first, lifted her suitcase from the trunk, and set it gently on the curb.

She hesitated, caught in the space between staying and going.

Holden stepped closer. One arm slid around her waist.

His other hand reached up and brushed a strand of hair from her face.

The goodbye gathered behind her ribs, aching with everything she didn't know how to say.

"Someone told me once," he said, voice low but sure, "that you don't really take your life back... until you move through what makes you want to run."

He didn't look at her right away.

His gaze drifted past her, somewhere far off—like he was standing in two places at once.

"When I needed it most," he added, softer now, "those were the words that got through."

She didn't speak. She didn't have to.

She saw it in the way his throat tightened, in the way his jaw worked to stay still.

This cost him something to share.

But his eyes—when they finally met hers—held steady.

He believed it. With every part of him. Because he'd lived it.

He didn't say who'd told him—but she could tell it had come during a moment that mattered.

"You deserve that too," he said gently.

Her throat tightened.

"If you ever need someone to talk to, or just... sit beside you—call."

He didn't say it out of obligation. It was unprompted. Offered like a lifeline.

He kissed her then. Slow. Intentional. A promise.

She pulled back. "I'll text when I land."

She turned toward the terminal doors.

She didn't look back.

But she felt him—still standing there—as they slid closed behind her.

Her team was already near the check-in counter.

Blake spotted her first. His gaze skimmed her face, the doors, then back again. A smirk tugged at his mouth.

"Please tell me he has a sister."

The laugh rose before she could stop it. It didn't lift the burden, but it loosened its grip.

Leave it to Blake to steady her without even trying.

The flights were smooth. She and Blake sat together, the hum of altitude creating space for what mattered.

They joked about food—his obsession with Coq au Vin, her refusal to try escargot. He teased her about her ever-growing list of "restaurants she says she'll try."

It was easy. Familiar. Safe.

Later, she turned toward him, more reflective.

"I think we just closed the biggest project of our careers," she said, glancing at the window.

Blake leaned back, arms folded. "Think?"

She smiled. "We did."

"And it held because you stepped in."

He shrugged. Not modest, just honest. "We built something good. Don't downplay your part."

She nodded. Gratitude didn't need more than that.

The plane landed. Luggage was claimed. Quick goodbyes exchanged with tired waves.

Outside the terminal, San Francisco greeted her with brisk, damp air. Fog wrapped the rooftops, blurring the skyline.

Everything moved faster here. The drone of engines. The distant sirens. No salt, no marsh. Charleston had vanished in the noise.

The drive to Hayes Valley was slow—rhythmic traffic, Muni clangs, crosswalk chirps. The city churned on, indifferent.

When she stepped into the apartment, the scent of Maddie's favorite fall candle met her—cinnamon, clove, orange peel.

"Maddie?" she called, hopeful.

No answer.

She rounded the corner into the kitchen, dragging her suitcase.

"Maddie?"

Then she saw her.

Maddie stood at the island. Not stiff—just... emptied out. Her jaw was set. Her eyes unreadable.

Eve's stomach flipped.

"Mads?"

No response.

Maddie slid something across the counter.

The pregnancy test.

Eve's breath caught.

Her mouth opened.

Maddie spoke first. "Is this real?"

"I didn't—"

"I was looking for earrings," Maddie said. "You said I could borrow them. You said I could look."

Eve remembered. She hadn't thought twice.

"I didn't mean for you to—"

"How long?"

The question gutted her.

Maddie's voice broke. "How long have you known?"

Too long.

"You let me talk about everything—Jax, work, stupid routines—and you sat there. Like nothing was happening."

"It wasn't like that."

"No?" Maddie's voice trembled. "Because it feels like you shut me out on purpose."

"I wasn't ready."

"I've been here," she said, her words clipped. "Every damn day. And you still lied."

Eve's voice dropped. "Because saying it made it real."

Silence fell.

"Well," Maddie breathed. "It's real now. And I can't do this tonight."

She turned and walked away.

The door slammed behind her.

Eve stood frozen, the chill from outside finally settling into her bones.

She waited, breath held, hoping the door would open again.

It didn't.

She rolled her suitcase to her room. Closed the door behind her.

The picture on her nightstand stared back—college graduation. Maddie's arm looped in hers, laughter frozen in time.

She dropped onto the bed, clutched a pillow, and cried until her chest ached.

There was nothing elegant about how she fell apart—

only grief.

That was the price of hiding secrets.

Chapter Sixteen

The next morning, sunlight spilled across her bedroom wall—pale, golden, unbothered. But the air felt thick, as if something sacred had snapped.

She wasn't sure when sleep had come. Jet lag hadn't been enough to quiet her mind. Hours passed replaying the confrontation—Maddie's voice cracking, the test sliding across the counter, the slam of the door.

She must have cried herself to sleep.

Now, her eyes were swollen, raw at the corners. Her body ached from the way she'd curled into herself, bracing against the grief like a shield.

The quiet felt foreign. Too gentle for what still churned inside her.

Regret crept in sharp, tracing the edge of fresh tears. She should've told Maddie. Trusted her sooner.

And if this was how Maddie responded—what would her parents say?

She reached for her phone, the screen lighting up in her palm.

No new messages.

Then it hit her.

She never texted Holden.

Eve: I made it home. I'm sorry I didn't text. Maddie found out. It got... ugly.

She didn't expect him to fix it. She wanted him to know.

The rest of the day moved like fog—slow and impenetrable.

Near midday, Eve cracked her door, hopeful the weight in the apartment had shifted. Maddie was in the kitchen, back turned, rinsing a mug in the sink.

"Hey," Eve tried, voice tentative. "Can we talk?"

Maddie didn't look up. Didn't speak.

She dried the mug, placed it gently on the shelf, and walked past Eve without a word—disappearing into her room.

The quiet that followed wasn't silence. It was distance.

Eve stood there a moment longer, then retreated to her room.

She didn't eat. Slept in broken intervals. Her body

heavy. Her thoughts heavier.

That night, just as she reached for the lamp, her phone

buzzed.

A single message from Holden:

Holden: Thanks for telling me.

No advice. No questions. No pressure.

Just presence.

And for tonight, that was enough.

By Monday, it had been eight days since Charleston.

Halloween had come and gone. November rolled in

with cooler nights and early dusk.

She packed away the Ashcroft files—neat folders, closed tabs, one drawer that slid shut with finality.

It should've felt like closure. Like the end of a chapter.

Instead, something sacred slipped from her grasp.

Her thoughts kept circling back to that Ashcroft presentation—those polished family photos. An unacknowledged presence. Like a note out of tune.

There were no new projects. No meetings. Only time.

Once, that felt like a luxury. Now it felt like exposure.

She stayed busy—reorganized her desk, deleted old emails, rearranged her books—anything to avoid sitting still long enough to feel it.

At night, she lay awake, staring at the ceiling, replaying the moment. The drawer. The missed opportunities.

And looming over her was the one conversation she couldn't escape.

Her parents.

They couldn't discover it by accident.

It had to come from her.

Her body was changing.

Slowly. Subtly.

She guessed she was twelve to thirteen weeks along.

One article said peach-sized. That made it harder to pretend.

She'd even typed abortion into a search bar once. The word stung—sharp and final.

Not because she didn't believe in the right to choose.

But because something inside her... couldn't make that choice.

So she thought about adoption.

She emailed an agency. Their reply came within a day. She opened it. Closed it. Opened it again.

Choosing a family. Telling her story. What if her story shaped the baby's life before it ever had a chance?

She hated the thought, but it lived in her.

She'd even considered keeping it, once. But what would that mean—for her future, her career, her sense of self?

She wasn't ready to decide.

But the choices waited, just the same.

A week had passed. Halloween had come and gone...

Decorations subtly shifted, store windows dressed for the holidays, as the city leaned into celebration. But inside the apartment, time hung suspended—no music, no laughter. Two ghosts moving through what used to feel like home.

Eve kept to her room. Clung to the workweek like a raft.

But the silence?

That hurt worse than yelling ever could.

She remembered something Maddie once said: I don't give second chances.

She used to admire that.

Now it gutted her.

Eve felt hollow inside it.

The bruises had faded, but a deeper ache replaced them. The kind she wasn't sure would ever fully heal.

Holden remained a steady presence.

Unobtrusive.

His texts arrived like breath—quiet, rhythmic, dependable.

Thinking of you. Hope today feels a little lighter. No pressure—just here.

Simple words. Nothing demanding. But they grounded her.

A ledge to rest on when everything else felt like freefall.

One night, much later than usual, another message came.

Longer. Different.

Holden: Sometimes I listen to instrumental music because it lets me feel without words getting in the way. It's a safe place for memory to surface—like giving your heart a chance to breathe before your mind catches up.

She read it twice. Then again.

Her mind wandered—to his car, the music playing low, the gentle way it filled the silence.

She hadn't thought much of it then.

But now... she could feel it. The intention behind it.

A quiet offering from someone who knew pain intimately, even if he hadn't said how.

He hadn't pried. Hadn't filled the silence with empty comfort. Just... gave her something. A small piece of his own way through.

And in this new, quiet ache she carried, it was enough to ease her shoulders.

Just a little.

Eight long days had passed since Maddie found the test.

November had rolled in, the city slipping into cooler nights and early dusk. Life outside moved forward, but inside the apartment, time stretched unbearably long, threatening to swallow her whole.

Maddie hadn't spoken to her. Not once.

She made it clear she wasn't ready—leaving rooms when Eve entered, shutting doors with soft finality, picking up extra shifts at work.

The distance cut deeper than the anger.

Eve sat on the edge of her bed, holding the photo from graduation. "I'm sorry," she said, thumb grazing the glass.

Holden's voice returned to her—soft, low: Move through the uncomfortable.

She couldn't take the isolation any longer.

It had settled into her bones, stretching each minute into something agonizing.

She had to try.

The hallway carried the scent of pumpkin—warm, spiced, comforting.

She followed it until she reached the kitchen.

Maddie stood at the counter, sleeves pushed up, stirring something in a bowl. Her shoulders were tight.

Eve hovered. "Maddie?"

She didn't respond, but she didn't walk away either.

Eve stepped closer. Her hand gripped the counter.

She let the words spill out. Broken. Bare.

"It was an assault."

The room fell silent, as if time had stopped.

The words hung in the air, fragile and irreversible.

Tears spilled down Eve's cheeks before she could stop them.

Maddie stood, spoon paused mid-stir. She didn't turn. Just... frozen.

Seconds passed. One. Then another. Long enough for Eve to believe it might be over—that maybe the words hadn't reached her, or worse, that they had.

Maybe this was the end of everything.

Then, slowly, Maddie turned.

Her expression shifted—first confusion, then something closer to heartbreak. Her eyes moved across Eve's face, searching, uncertain.

She didn't reach out right away.

And then she stepped forward. Closed the space between them.

Her arms came around Eve, not tight, not certain. But there.

Eve collapsed into her, the sobs breaking free, shattering whatever wall remained.

They stood like that for a long moment, wrapped in something too raw to name. Not forgiveness. Not yet.

But not hiding either.

Later, they sat at the kitchen island. The pendant light cast a soft halo on the counter between them.

Maddie was the first to speak. Her voice carried something raw. "Why didn't you tell me?"

It wasn't anger. It was something more complex—a question wrapped in sadness.

Eve didn't hesitate.

"It wasn't you," she said, her voice catching. "I swear it wasn't because I didn't trust you."

She blinked hard. "It was me. I was scared. And the longer I waited, the harder it got. I kept thinking—if I said it out loud, I'd lose everything. That no one would stay."

Maddie's gaze didn't waver. "I would never leave you."

Eve swallowed hard and nodded. "I know that now. But I didn't believe it then. I couldn't."

She exhaled, like an unspooling thread.

She told Maddie everything —how the alley had changed everything. She described the test in the bathroom, the hollow panic that followed, and the weeks of barely holding on.

And Holden.

She told it, piece by piece, giving Maddie the whole picture.

Maddie didn't interrupt. Didn't ask for clarification or more details. She listened. Her fingers wrapped around her mug, knuckles white, but she didn't flinch.

When the story was done, a long pause filled the space between them. Not awkward. Just full.

Then Maddie said softly, "Holden knows?"

Eve nodded. "He found out... not long after I collapsed. It wasn't how I planned. But he's been..." she trailed off, searching. "Kind."

Maddie looked down, then back at her. Her voice wasn't cold, but it carried a bittersweet tone.

"I'm glad someone was there for you."

Eve's chest clenched.

"I wish it had been me."

It hurt, but not in a way that required defense, because she understood.

"Me too," Eve said honestly. "But I didn't even know how to be there for myself."

Maddie looked at her, and Eve saw the same girl who'd stood beside her since freshman year of college—the one who'd made ramen taste like a feast and turned dorm rooms into safety. She was still there. Hurt, yes. But not gone.

This wasn't the end.

But it was a fresh start.

The afternoon melted into evening.

They moved through the apartment not as strangers, circling each other in recognizable rhythms. Maddie washed dishes. Eve folded laundry.

Dinner was takeout, eaten together without ceremony.

Outside, the sky faded into a gray hue.

Eve reached for another piece of garlic bread, Maddie spoke—gently, but directly.

"How far along are you?"

Eve looked up.

"I'm not sure. Maybe thirteen weeks. I haven't seen a doctor yet."

"Have you told your parents?"

She shook her head.

"No. I've been hiding from everyone."

Eve answered what she could, admitted what she hadn't done, and shared what she didn't know.

Her expression didn't change; there was no judgment, only acknowledgment of the burden.

Not forgiveness.

But something like grace.

Before bed, Maddie paused in her bedroom doorway.

"It hurt that you lied. I don't understand all of it…"

She paused.

"I want to move on from this. But it won't be easy. It'll take some time."

Eve nodded. "I understand."

Maddie stepped inside her room and let the door close behind her.

Eve stood there for a breath longer.

For the first time in days, something inside her began to loosen.

With each person who knew, she felt a little lighter.

Exposed, yes—but also free.

She hadn't expected that when this all began.

She hadn't dared.

In the hush of her room, Eve sat on the edge of her bed, phone in hand.

Outside, the city remained draped in fog, but inside her, something had cleared.

She opened Holden's thread and typed:

Eve: We talked. It wasn't easy... but it helped. It's a start.

His reply came almost instantly:

Holden: Proud of you. That's a tremendous step.

She exhaled.

Then slid beneath the covers and switched off the light.

In the darkness, she stared at the muted outline of her ceiling.

She didn't know who she'd be by the time she reached the end of this journey.

But for the first time, she didn't feel alone.

And for now, that gave her a little hope.

Chapter Seventeen

Maddie's discovery of her secret had already caused devastation. Now, in the first week of November, the slow, intentional work of repair had begun. Holden carried the weight of what he knew. But their parents—the ones who had poured everything into them, who relied on their composure, who trusted them with their name—still had no idea.

This truth couldn't be left to chance. It had to come from her.

They began carefully, picking through the broken pieces.

Dinner at the same table. The same shows humming in the background. A laugh now and then. It wasn't what it had been—and maybe it never would be—but it was something. A beginning.

The apartment felt quieter now. Not healed. Not whole. But softer somehow.

One night, Maddie tucked her legs beneath her on the couch, a mug of peppermint tea in hand.

"I had the weirdest install this week," she said, unprompted.

Eve glanced up from her laptop, caught off guard but grateful.

"This boutique in Pacific Heights? Ultra-minimalist. Total perfectionists. They sent the wrong product line for the fall window—florals and pastels. In *October.*"

She raised an eyebrow.

Eve smirked. "Let me guess... they loved it."

"They freaked out at first. But traffic doubled. Some influencer tagged it an 'anti-seasonal rebellion.' Now the owner thinks she's a genius."

Eve laughed. "That sounds like your kind of chaos."

Maddie grinned, then looked down into her mug. "Yeah. It was actually kind of fun."

The warmth stretched between them for a moment before settling into a gentler silence. Maddie was here. She was talking again. But Eve could still feel the caution—the softened edges of a friend slowly rebuilding herself.

Still, she was trying.

And Eve didn't push. She just let the moment rest between them like a truce neither had spoken aloud.

Maddie spent more evenings with Jax now, but she never used the distance as a wedge.

Eve noticed the way her face softened when he texted. The way her laughter came more easily around him.

Once, Eve glimpsed them curled on the couch, a blanket draped across their legs, a movie flickering in the dark, their laughter braided into something whole.

A sharp pang caught in her chest. Not resentment— just something unshakably lonely.

Maddie didn't press her. But she left breadcrumbs.

A folded list of OBGYNs, circled in pink highlighter.

A forwarded article: *Ten Baby Books That Don't Suck.*

A sticky note on the fridge: *Clementines help. I bought extra.*

They weren't conversations. But they were gestures.

Signals that said: *I see you. I'm trying. I need space too.*

Eve felt the shift in her body. Her energy was steadier now, the morning nausea gone. Her skin had taken on that second-trimester glow she'd read about, and her belly had started to swell—just enough that certain shirts no longer worked.

She didn't hide at home. Not from Maddie.

But outside? She wasn't ready to be seen. Not yet.

Still, she couldn't ignore it anymore.

And maybe—she didn't want to.

Midweek, her father sent a text:

Dad: *Coffee? Just us. Friday morning?*

She stared at the message longer than she meant to.

They'd had hundreds of work lunches, debriefs, and campaign reviews. But this felt different.

He chose a small café tucked downtown—wood-paneled, espresso-scented, and lined with used paperbacks. The kind of place where conversations felt real.

She shed her coat and settled across from him, hands wrapped around a mug of peppermint tea—gentler than coffee, grounding in a way nothing else was.

"You crushed the Ashcroft project," he said.

She blinked.

"Hayes and Eliza Ashcroft sent a handwritten note. Said you exceeded expectations. That the rollout felt seamless—rooted in trust. *Their* words."

That project had been her anchor. She'd completed it mid-collapse—held it together with trembling hands and a fraying heart.

"I couldn't have done it without Blake."

"Blake's solid. But the leadership? That was you."

She looked down, unsure how to receive it.

"You've found your rhythm," he added. "And I want your next project to reflect that."

Her gaze lifted, cautious.

"You pick it," he said. "Build it. Lead it. You've earned that."

The words landed with quiet weight. Not like pressure. Like possibility.

He smiled. "You remember coming to the office when you were little? Clipboard in hand, telling my team they needed more color in the mock-ups?"

Her mouth curved. "I do."

"You were right, by the way."

She laughed softly, eyes glassy now.

"I'm proud of you," he said. "Not just for the work. For how you carry it."

She swallowed hard. "Thank you."

He lifted his cup in a small salute. "You're building something that lasts."

They sat for a moment in the hum of the café.

She wasn't sure how she was still standing—not with everything she carried.

But maybe strength wasn't loud. Or even confident.

Maybe the strongest thing you could do was simply keep going—especially when you felt broken.

That evening, Eve paused in the doorway to the living room.

Maddie looked up from her phone.

"I thought maybe we could stay in tonight?" Eve asked. "Order from that place on 19th?"

Maddie nodded. "Yeah. Okay."

They ordered garlic bread, thick pasta, and Maddie's favorite red—mint tea for Eve. The smell of basil and toasted cheese filled the apartment with a kind of comfort that didn't need explanation.

They were content in each other's company.

Halfway through the meal, Eve pushed her plate aside.

"I need to tell them."

Maddie looked up.

"My parents," Eve clarified. "Before Thanksgiving."

Maddie gave a slow nod.

"It scares me," Eve added. "Not because I think they'll be cruel... but because I waited. I let it get this far."

"They might be hurt," Maddie said gently. "But they'll still love you."

Eve looked down. "I remember getting a B on a math test in seventh grade. My dad didn't even say anything—just looked disappointed. And in fourth grade, I missed a line in a school play. My mom didn't come backstage afterward."

"They're human," Maddie offered. "And so are you."

A pause.

Then Maddie smiled, trying to shift the tone. "Jax spilled an entire glass of wine trying to impress me with a card trick."

Eve snorted. "No."

"Ruined the whole table. Still tried to say it was 'part of the trick.'"

The laugh helped. Her fear didn't press so tightly.

It wasn't gone. But it gave her some room to breathe.

Eve's voice remained steady. "I've ruled out one thing. I won't get an abortion."

Maddie waited.

"It's not something I can do. I've thought about it… really thought about it. But it's not for me."

Maddie shifted forward slightly, listening.

"I've thought about adoption," Eve continued. "It's not a decision yet. But it's something I keep circling back to."

"You don't have to explain it to me," Maddie said.

"I want to be honest."

"When will you tell them?"

Eve hesitated. "Before Thanksgiving. If I wait any longer, I'll lose the nerve."

Maddie studied her. "Do you want me to go with you?"

Eve's heart kicked. "You'd do that?"

Maddie nodded. "Yeah. You shouldn't have to do that alone."

It caught Eve off guard—tender and unexpected.

Not everything was healed.

But something inside her softened. A step forward.

The weekend arrived wrapped in gray. Mist clung to the sidewalks. Tree branches dripped over parked cars. The air had a chill that bit through her sleeves.

Eve didn't do much—answered emails, made soup, cleaned out her closet. It was a typical day. A calm one. And that felt good.

That evening, Maddie left with Jax. Something casual, she'd said. They paused at the door, laughing softly. Eve smiled, but it didn't quite reach.

The apartment, once empty with avoidance, now felt empty with absence.

Eve curled on the couch, blanket over her lap, the heater humming faintly in the corner.

She felt Holden's absence too. The way his hand on her lower back could steady her.

They talked most nights now. Not always about anything important. But enough.

Tonight, when she meant to text, her thumb slipped.

Video call.

His face filled the screen.

Unshaven. Tired. Still achingly handsome.

"Hey," he said, voice soft. "Pleasant surprise."

"Meant to text," she smiled.

"I'm glad you didn't."

The lamplight behind him was warm, but his features looked drawn. His voice, quieter than usual.

She noticed a cardboard box on the coffee table. Half-open. Something about it felt... wrong. Like a drawer left open in a room you hadn't meant to enter.

"What's that?" she asked.

Holden's eyes followed hers. His posture shifted slightly.

"Some old family stuff. Cleaning out a few things."

His tone didn't invite questions.

She didn't press. Just pivoted.

"I'm telling them," she said. "My parents. Friday before Thanksgiving."

His gaze locked on hers.

"That's brave," he said.

She shook her head. "It's necessary."

He tilted his head. "You're taking your life back."

"I'm trying."

"No," he said softly. "You're doing it."

She saw the fatigue in his eyes. The way his shoulders sank into the couch.

"Get some sleep," she said gently. "We'll talk tomorrow."

She hesitated before ending the call.

Then she folded the blanket and walked to her bedroom.

Opened the desk drawer.

Took out her planner.

She marked the Friday before Thanksgiving in bright
red ink.

That would be the day she told them.

When one more fractured piece of truth found its
place.

Chapter Eighteen

The city felt sharp that Saturday morning—streets arranged in a precise grid, glass towers catching the sun like polished knives. There was order here.

Inside the apartment, Eve moved with similar care—watching, listening, deciding. It had been a week since her father offered her the chance to choose her next project. The days since had unfolded without fanfare. Even normalcy had crept in: morning tea, quiet emails, peaceful dinners. Outside, Thanksgiving prep had begun to show—shop windows dressed in muted gold and burnt orange. The air was crisp and damp, the scent of fog clinging to everything.

She hadn't rushed.

Early in the week, her father sent over a folder of project leads: boutique hospitality groups, regional expansions, and a nonprofit theatre initiative based in Sausalito.

Eve waited until today to take a closer look. She wanted space—intentional time to feel something resonate.

The Crescent Theatre caught her attention.

A modest rebrand. But behind it, a mission: to bring art programs to low-income families and revive a corner of the community that still valued beauty.

Small in scope. Full of heart.

She didn't hesitate. She typed the email:

I'll take the community theatre project. It feels like the right fit.

His reply came instantly:

Proud of you. Run with it. Let me know what you need.

A small reclaiming. A quiet win.

She closed the laptop and leaned back, her palm resting over the soft curve of her stomach. The swell was more defined now—enough to shift her silhouette, enough to require different clothes. The kind of change that no longer hid in shadows.

By Wednesday night, she was in bed, the phone warm in her hand. She scrolled past her mom's name once. Then again. Then hovered—hesitated—and pressed "Call."

It rang once.

"Sweetheart?" Her mom's voice came quickly—bright, surprised, tinged with concern. "Is everything okay?"

Guilt tightened in Eve's chest. She hadn't reached out since before July.

"Yeah," Eve said. "I wanted to... catch up. I remember saying once the Ashcroft project was over, I'd come up for air. And here I am."

Her mother's voice softened. "I'm so glad to hear that. You've been missed."

"I was wondering..." Eve cleared her throat. "If we could do dinner next Friday. The three of us. Before the holidays get crazy."

A pause. Eve held her breath.

"Oh, honey," her mom exhaled. "That sounds wonderful. I'd love that."

Eve's hand trembled. "I thought it'd be nice. It's been too long."

"I've been worried," her mom admitted. "You seemed so overwhelmed. I kept telling myself it was just work, but..."

"I'm okay now," Eve said. "Things are settling."

"I'll make something cozy," her mom said, brightening. "Maybe that lemon risotto you love?"

"Yeah," Eve whispered, guilt pressing deeper. "That sounds perfect."

They said their goodbyes, and when Eve set the phone down, she let her body finally relax.

Maddie had offered to come. But Eve understood now—this moment had to be hers. Her parents deserved that.

Thursday afternoon, the apartment smelled of brown sugar and cinnamon.

Maddie was in the kitchen, the clatter of mixing bowls and hum of the hand mixer weaving through the softened air.

Eve sat curled on the couch, a blanket across her lap. The swelling beneath her ribs pulled her forward— tight, but not painful. Her body was preparing.

"Did you look at any of the doctors I recommended?" Maddie asked. Her tone was light, but there was intent behind it.

"I skimmed," Eve said. "There's one—Dr. Vega—that looked promising."

Maddie turned. "That's the one I thought you'd pick. She's sharp. Doesn't talk down to you. That's what the reviews said."

Eve hesitated. "I called my mom last night."

"Oh?"

"I asked if we could have dinner. Just us. Next Friday."

Maddie wiped her hands on a towel. "That's soon."

"It needed to be," Eve said. "If I wait, I'll lose the nerve."

Maddie nodded. "Do you want me to go with you?"

Eve shook her head. "Thank you, but no. They need to hear it from me."

No tension. Just something tender in the silence between them.

"I spoke to someone at the adoption agency," Eve said. "They'll need paperwork from a doctor before anything can move forward."

Maddie sat beside her—close, but not touching. "You're moving forward," she said. "That's what matters."

"I'll call a doctor soon," Eve said. "I just... need a moment to catch my breath."

Maddie nodded once. "Then take your breath. And make the call."

That night, Eve called Holden.

It rang three times before he picked up—longer than usual.

"Hey," he said, voice soft but distant. "Sorry. You caught me mid-cleanup."

She heard rustling—papers maybe, or boxes. Not the usual stillness behind him.

She didn't mention it.

"I scheduled it," she said. "The dinner. Next Friday."

"That's not just big. That's brave," he said. "How do you feel?"

"Scared."

"You're allowed to be."

A breath.

"I've been thinking about my options," she said.

He didn't interrupt.

"I thought about it," she admitted, voice low.

"Abortion."

She heard his breath catch.

"But I couldn't do it. Even now... I can't."

His voice, when it came, was gentle. "You didn't owe me that. But thank you."

"I'm leaning toward adoption. I've started gathering info. Nothing final."

A pause.

"Did you ever think about keeping it?" he asked, barely audible.

Eve blinked. "Not really. I wouldn't know how to explain it—to the baby, or myself."

He waited, then said, "You don't have to have all the answers right now. You're allowed to feel joy in this too. Even if it came from something awful. Even if people wouldn't understand."

Eve's chest tightened. "I don't know if I can."

"You will. Or you won't. But that's yours to decide."

"I need to see a doctor," she said. "Maddie recommended Dr. Vega."

"Good. That's good."

But something in his voice shifted—cooler, thinner.

"You okay?" she asked.

"Yeah. Just... rough week. High-maintenance client."

But it didn't sound like work.

"If you want to talk—"

"I know."

A pause.

"I should go," she said.

"Me too."

The call ended. The quiet lingered.

It wasn't fatigue she heard in him. Something was shifting beneath the surface.

She opened her laptop. Searched Dr. Vega's name.

Monday, November 24th. 8:00 a.m.

She booked it.

The confirmation arrived seconds later.

She closed the screen and let the moment settle in her bones.

By Friday night, she felt steadier.

She had chosen a project. Scheduled the dinner. Made the appointment.

For the first time in months, she was moving forward.

After everything, that felt like hope.

Chapter Nineteen

Late Friday afternoon. Beyond her office window, the city was already sliding into twilight.

Eve sat at her desk. A soft hum rose from the floor below, a steady presence beneath her. Papers were stacked neatly, her planner tucked beside her keyboard. She slowly shut her laptop, her thoughts drifting as she reached for her coat.

She'd called her mom the Wednesday before—giving herself more than a week to settle her nerves, to shape a plan, to breathe through the fear.

But all she'd really done was imagine a hundred ways to back out.

Still, things had moved forward. She'd finalized her agreement with Crescent Theatre earlier that week— her first chosen project. A modest rebrand designed to boost community engagement and support youth programs. Small in scale, but rooted in purpose. Strategy calls were already scheduled for the following week. No team. Just her.

With the appointment set for Monday, there was only one hurdle left—tonight.

The evening arrived colder than expected.

Low clouds smeared the skyline. The city teetered on the edge of winter, that seasonless blur of rain and wind and early dark. Eve had left the office shortly after four, stopping at a corner florist on her walk home. She picked out lilies and eucalyptus—her mom's favorites.

Back at the flat, she moved through the living room, rearranging the bouquet on the console table for the third time, trying to burn off the nervous energy coiling in her chest. She wore jeans and a soft blouse that clung gently to her changing shape.

Maddie sat on the couch, chin on her knees, watching her. "You're not hiding it," she said gently.

Eve looked down. The curve was undeniable now.

"Not here," she said. "I don't want to hide here."

Maddie nodded, recognizing the effort in Eve's voice. The way she was fidgeting, rehearsing invisible words.

"They're going to love you through this," Maddie said, rising slowly and stepping into the space beside her. She touched Eve's arm. "You know that, right?"

"I didn't just hide it." Her voice caught. "I lied. Repeatedly."

"I know," Maddie said softly. "Believe me, I know how that feels."

Eve looked over, surprised.

"I lied to you, too. Where I was going, what I suspected. I know what it's like to be on both sides—hurt, angry, trying to rebuild something you're not sure can be rebuilt."

She pulled Eve into a gentle hug. The kind of hug you give when you're still figuring out trust.

"But you're telling them now. That matters."

Eve nodded against her shoulder.

Maddie leaned back with a faint smile. "Besides, you're their only child. They don't have a backup option."

A breath caught in Eve's throat—half laugh, half sob. "That's your version of comfort?"

Maddie shrugged. "Just playing the odds."

Eve smiled. It wasn't much, but it helped.

"I hope you're right."

"I usually am," Maddie said. "Eventually."

She stepped back slightly. "Are you sure you don't want me to come with you?"

Eve hesitated, but the answer was firm. "It has to be me. Just me."

A pause.

"I confirmed the appointment," Eve added. "Dr. Vega. After Thanksgiving."

Maddie's face softened. "I hope you like her."

Eve reached for her sweater and slipped into her shoes.

Maddie followed to the door, resting her hand briefly on the knob. "Call me if you need me."

"I will."

One more hug. Closer this time.

There was still healing to do—but they were finding their way.

Eve stepped out into the night. The bouquet cradled in one arm. Her keys cold in her hand. Every step toward her parents' house felt heavier—but steadier, too.

The drive dragged.

Rain tapped against the windshield, each drop loud in the silent car. Headlights smeared the road like unfinished thoughts.

She turned onto her parents' street. Everything looked the same.

Porch garlands. Amber bulbs. Chrysanthemums in rust and gold lining the walkway. A wreath of dried leaves, perfectly centered on the front door.

Picture-perfect. As always.

And suddenly, that perfection felt like a threat. Like a place she no longer belonged.

She remembered coming home junior year, after blanking on her AP Chem presentation. Spiraling. Her parents had seen right through her. Her mom sat

beside her. Her dad made tea. They let her fall apart,

then helped her piece it back together.

That memory loosened something in her chest. They'd

shown up for her before.

But this was different.

The bouquet trembled in her hands as she reached the

steps.

She paused at the door, bracing herself.

Her mom opened it before Eve could knock, as if she'd

known.

"Sweetheart," she said, eyes brightening. She pulled

her in without hesitation.

Eve melted into the embrace—unexpectedly grateful for it.

"These are for you," she said, offering the bouquet.

Her mom's face lit up. "You always know what I love."

Inside, the house smelled of cinnamon and lemon. Pumpkins lined the staircase. Candles flickered in amber jars. A wreath of dried oranges and pinecones adorned the dining room wall.

It all came rushing back—eight years old, stealing sugar cookies, her mom humming to old jazz. But the warmth faded just as quickly. Would this house still feel like home after tonight?

She followed her mom into the kitchen. Her dad stood at the stove, stirring something savory.

Her mom pulled out a scalloped vase. "Remember how you used to rearrange the store bouquets before checkout?"

Eve laughed. "I think the florists hated me."

"They hated how much better you made them look," her dad chimed in.

"You always say that," she said, smiling.

"You still have time," he said with a wink.

Her mom wiped her hands. "How's work?"

Eve took a seat at the island. "I signed on to lead the Crescent Theatre rebrand."

"A great spot in Sausalito," her dad said, brightening.

"They want to rebuild support—more funding for low-income arts programs."

"Good bones," he said. "Needs heart. You'll give it that."

Her mom nodded. "You always do."

The rhythm between them helped. Like muscle memory.

But something still ached in her chest—something like longing. Or fear that she'd never have this again.

They talked about everything except the truth.

Her dad asked about strategy. Her mom pitched spring trips. They passed salad, poured sparkling water, and laughed—just like always.

It was almost worse that it felt so normal.

Back in college, coming home for the weekend felt like a reset. The things she brought home then were small. Cracks.

This was a fracture.

And there was no easy way across it.

She picked at her food. Smiled at the right times. But the weight in her chest was growing, pressing against her ribs.

After dinner came apple pecan bars—her favorite. Her mom slid one across the table with a smile. Eve nodded. But her stomach was too tight.

Talk shifted to Florence. A hidden winery. Flights in April. Her parents laughed and reminisced.

Eve sat too straight in the armchair. Half-listening, fully waiting. But the moment never came.

She couldn't let it pass.

Her dad noticed first.

Mid-laugh, he turned. Studied her posture. Her stillness. Her clenched hands.

"Eve?" he asked gently.

She looked up. His eyes were searching. That look—the one from childhood when he knew she was pretending.

Her chest hitched.

Her mom set down her coffee. "Sweetheart?"

Eve tried. "I…"

But the words broke apart.

Her breath stuttered. Her eyes filled. She pressed her palms to her thighs, trying to ground herself.

"I'm okay," she whispered. A lie.

"When I was in Charleston," she said, "in July—something happened."

They froze.

"I didn't tell anyone. I flew home. I pretended it was fine."

Silence.

"I was assaulted."

Her mom gasped, hand flying to her mouth.

Her dad's jaw clenched.

"I didn't go to the police. Or the hospital. I didn't understand what had happened. Not right away."

She looked up, vision swimming.

"I'm pregnant."

Her mom let out a soft, stunned sound. She reached for Eve, arms wrapping gently around her.

Eve collapsed into her. Trembling.

"I'm sorry," she cried. "I didn't want to disappoint you."

Her dad paced, trying to stay composed.

"I didn't want to bring shame. Or fear. Or ruin everything."

She wasn't sure how long they sat like that. Just that her mother didn't let go. And her father hadn't spoken.

When she could breathe again, Eve wiped her face.

"I'm figuring things out," she said. "Slowly."

"I'm not asking for anything."

Still, silence.

Then her mother: "Why didn't you come to us?"

"I was afraid. I thought you'd look at me differently."

"You thought we'd turn away from you?"

She couldn't answer.

Her dad's voice cracked. "You carried this alone?"

She nodded.

"And went to work. Led an alliance. Showed up to dinner."

He shook his head. "Unbelievable."

She braced—but it wasn't condemnation. Just sorrow.

Her mom wiped her own tears. "Thank you," she whispered. "For telling us. Finally."

Eve exhaled.

They were still here.

Still her parents.

Then—three sharp knocks.

They startled.

Her dad stood. "I wasn't expecting anyone."

"Probably a neighbor," her mom said. "Let your father

handle it."

He disappeared down the hallway.

He was gone too long.

When he returned, Holden followed.

Eve's breath caught.

He looked like someone who had walked through a

storm.

She stood and crossed to him. Folded into his chest without a word.

"I couldn't let you do it alone," he murmured.

She looked up. His face pale. Hollow.

Her dad's voice cut through. "Holden, would you join me in my office?"

Eve tensed.

"Of course," Holden said, eyes flicking to her.

Her mom wrapped an arm around her. "Come on," she said gently. "You and I have catching up to do."

Eve followed.

Toward all the things she couldn't hear.

When they returned, Holden greeted her mom with quiet sincerity. They sat together for a while longer, fresh cups of coffee passed between them.

No one spoke of what had been said.

But the room had shifted. Not tense—just full.

Eve curled into the couch, tired down to her bones.

"I should go," she said finally.

Holden stood. Her dad shook his hand. Her mom pulled him in for a hug.

Her mom kissed Eve's cheek. Her dad rested a hand on her head—just like when she was small.

No one repeated the words. But she felt them.

Still loved.

Still theirs.

Outside, the rain had sharpened. The air bit at her cheeks.

Holden stood beside her on the porch, hands in his coat pockets.

"Stay with me," he said. Not a question. A home.

She looked at him.

This man who had shown up.

And she didn't hesitate.

She took his hand.

And this time, she let herself lean in.

Chapter Twenty

The hotel suite was peaceful—the kind that welcomed the weary.

Spacious. Well-appointed. Elegant in a way that didn't clamor for attention.

Holden guided her inside with a gentle hand at her back. The door fell shut behind them, and Eve stepped forward, letting her lungs expand. The dinner, the tears, the weight of truth still lived in her bones—but for the first time in hours, she could breathe.

He was like that for her. Air.

She scanned the space slowly, eyes drifting across soft corners and muted textures.

"I'm going to check in with Maddie," she said, pulling her phone from her bag.

Holden nodded, slipping off his coat and draping it neatly over a chair.

In the bathroom, she closed the door behind her. The mirror caught her reflection—wind-bitten cheeks, exhaustion beneath her eyes, something frayed at the edges but still holding.

She dialed.

Maddie picked up on the second ring. "You alive?"

"I survived it," Eve said. "Somehow."

Jax's voice filtered in the background—soft laughter, faint music.

"I told them everything," Eve added. "All of it."

A pause. Then Maddie's voice shifted—gentler now.

"I'm so proud of you." There was real relief in it.

"I know Holden showed up," she added. "I gave him a warning. Just in case."

Eve smiled faintly. "Thank you. For having my back."

"Always," Maddie said, though her voice still carried a thread of cautiousness.

After they hung up, Eve lingered. Her gaze drifted to the curve of her belly in the mirror—more defined now.

She didn't know exactly who she was becoming.

But maybe—just maybe—it was someone stronger.

Back in the suite, dinner had arrived. He must've known she'd need something warm. Grounding.

The scent alone made her stomach tighten. She hadn't realized how hungry she was until now.

Holden gestured toward the small table. "Eat."

They sat beside each other and shared pasta with roasted vegetables. The stillness between them was comforting. The food was simple but satisfying. Her appetite surprised her.

Afterward, he offered her one of his T-shirts.

She changed in the bathroom, pulling it over her head. It hung low on her thighs—soft, worn, safe.

When she emerged, Holden had changed into flannel pants and a faded T-shirt, barefoot. There was something intimate about it. Not sexual. Not performative. Just... familiar.

They climbed into bed without ceremony. The warm lamplight spilled across the covers.

"You did something hard tonight," Holden said. "And you didn't run."

"It was terrifying," she admitted. "But also... freeing. Like I could finally exhale."

She turned toward him. "Maybe I'm not drowning anymore."

He reached for her hand, brushing his thumb across her knuckles. Then leaned in and pressed a kiss to her cheek. It wasn't pity. It was something steadier.

She let herself feel it.

A moment passed. Then, with a faint smile, she said, "I made my first doctor's appointment."

His brows lifted. "Yeah?"

"Monday."

He nodded slowly, like he was filing the detail away

somewhere permanent.

Their bodies aligned beneath the covers.

They fell asleep like that—limbs drawn close, holding

onto something neither could name yet.

Gray light filtered through the curtains like breath on

cold glass. The hum of the city stirred beneath it—

muffled engines, distant footsteps, the occasional

horn—all swallowed by the fog-heavy hush of a San

Francisco November.

Eve woke with Holden curled around her, steady and

protective, blankets tangled at their waists. She didn't

want to move. Not yet.

Eventually, they walked down to the bistro tucked in the lobby. The air outside was sharp with the season's turn.

They found a table near the window.

She picked at a blueberry scone, tea warming her hands. Holden scrolled the news on his phone with a coffee in hand. Outside, holiday wreaths went up in shop windows. Lights blinked behind frosted glass. The city had entered anticipation mode—perched at the edge of something festive.

And here they were—watching it unfold like a scene to witness, not yet join.

It felt... ordinary.

It felt good.

They returned to the apartment just before noon.

Laughter echoed from the living room.

Maddie and Jax were there.

And judging by the tangled blanket on the couch and

the two mugs in the sink, Jax had stayed over.

Eve shot Maddie a look. Maddie's cheeks flushed,

feigning innocence.

But beneath the grin was a moment—a flicker of

awareness. Maddie's gaze dipped to Eve's belly. A quiet

acknowledgment.

They all decided to wander downtown. The air was

crisp and electric. Street performers played under café

awnings. Families browsed pop-up markets. Boots

shuffled through fallen leaves.

They started at the Japanese Tea Garden, each clutching ceramic cups, fingers curled against the cold.

"Jax doesn't do tea," Maddie teased.

"Correction—I don't do tea this fancy," Jax replied, peering at the steam like it held secrets.

Holden chuckled. "I've seen him chug gas station green tea on road trips like it was electrolytes."

"That was medicinal," Jax said solemnly. "Someone—no names—made us eat questionable sushi off the back of a boat."

Holden raised a hand. "It was a dare."

"You dared yourself."

Maddie laughed so hard she nearly spilled her drink.

They wandered deeper into the garden, the conversation falling into easy rhythm. Golden leaves filtered the sunlight. Gravel crunched beneath their shoes.

Maddie pointed toward the koi pond. "We used to sneak into a park near campus. I'd bring snacks. Eve brought flashcards."

"She was probably the professor," Jax said. "No one knew it yet."

Eve rolled her eyes, but warmth spread across her cheeks.

Later, they stopped for lunch at The Foghorn. Wings. Cheese fries. The kind of food that tastes better after laughter.

Conversation ebbed and flowed—stories, teasing, a few quiet moments in between.

By the time dusk crept in, city lights flickered on one by one.

Outside the apartment, Maddie and Jax lingered on the steps. Eve and Maddie exchanged a glance. No words needed.

Holden's hand found the small of her back as they walked away.

Back at the suite, Eve moved slower.

The day had left its mark—ankles tight, back aching, a gentle stretch pulling across her belly.

She paused in the center of the room, letting herself feel it—the weight, the gratitude, the ache.

She looked at Holden.

And smiled.

Room service arrived—broth, warm bread, a bowl of greens.

They ate slowly. Legs tangled beneath the table. City lights blurred beyond the glass.

Holden leaned back, fingers tracing the rim of his glass. "I fly out early Tuesday," he said, watching her face.

Eve's chest tightened more than she expected.

She hesitated. "I don't want this to feel like pressure... but would you go with me? To the appointment?"

No pause. No calculation.

"Of course I will."

The answer settled something in her. Her eyes stung with the force of everything she wasn't saying.

He made a choice.

And it meant more than either of them said aloud.

Later, as dishes sat empty and the sky deepened, Holden turned to her.

"I want to show you something."

Eve followed him to the bed. He reached into his overnight bag and pulled out a worn photograph—creases at the corners, colors softened by time.

He handed it to her like it mattered.

Four teenagers on a beach. Two boys. Two girls.

Sunlight. Sand. Laughter frozen mid-frame.

Both boys bore matching tattoos—just above the bone.

Eve's breath caught.

"Me, Levi, Ivy, and Bella. Sixteen. Summer before senior year."

She traced a finger across the photo.

This wasn't the first time she'd seen Levi. That Christmas photo on Holden's shelf... but this was different. Older. More defined. Still unmistakably him.

"You were happy," she said.

"We were," Holden replied. A smile flickered and vanished.

He told her about sneaking off to get tattoos. A dare. A shared secret.

The memory stirred a soft laugh—but it rang thin.

She watched his face. There was love. But also distance. Like the joy had calcified into something painful to carry.

He'd said *were*, not *are*.

She wanted to ask what happened that summer.

But she didn't.

Truth had to be offered—not extracted.

So instead, she leaned in and kissed his cheek.

"Thank you," she whispered. "For letting me see that part of you."

Holden studied her face. Like trying to memorize it.

They climbed into bed without another word.

Her head found his chest. His arm looped around her

waist. The lamplight wrapped them in quiet.

For a while, they just were.

Then, his voice cut through.

"That summer changed everything."

His hand moved in slow circles along her spine.

She didn't press.

So she kissed the spot over his heart.

She wasn't sure if he needed comfort—but her instinct

told her to stay.

He pulled her closer.

His breath caught, then evened.

And for the second night in a row, they let the silence

speak for them.

Not out of fear.

But because something real was taking root.

Something fragile.

And for now, that was enough.

Chapter Twenty-One

Sunday unfurled with simple, steady rhythms that made everything feel stable again.

They slept in—wrapped in layers and quiet. Breakfast was slow: coffee, scrambled eggs, and fruit eaten in bed with conversation kept light. Neither pressed for more than the day could offer.

By mid-morning, Eve returned to the apartment. Her body needed rest. Holden stayed at the suite, citing emails he needed to answer. At the door, he kissed her forehead and promised, "I'll see you in the morning."

Monday arrived brisk and sharp, the kind of morning that slid under collars and cuffs without warning. Winter was whispering now—early, gray, inevitable.

Eve pulled her coat tighter as she approached Dr. Vega's office.

The city stirred with its practiced rhythm—coffee carts clattering into place, traffic lights blinking like slow pulses, fog slipping between rooftops and lamp posts. Life moved forward, indifferent.

Holden waited outside, hands tucked in his coat pockets. He offered her a quiet smile and opened the door.

The waiting room buzzed in a gentle, continuous hum. Pregnant women filled the space—some waiting, some pacing, some reading pamphlets or scrolling their phones. A stroller creaked as a sleeping infant shifted. Behind one door, the sound of laughter filtered through from a prenatal class.

Eve checked in at the front desk, where a receptionist smiled warmly and handed her a clipboard.

"Go ahead and fill this out. We'll call you shortly."

She nodded and sat beside Holden, completing the form with practiced ease—until she reached one question.

Father's health history.

Her pen stilled. A flash of memory—of July—rushed in sharp and unwanted.

She skipped the question.

"Eve Whitmore?" a nurse called gently.

She glanced at Holden. He rose and followed without hesitation.

The exam room was small and brightly lit, the air tinged with antiseptic and lemon. On the wall, a diagram of fetal development. Below it, neat shelves of pamphlets and plastic models.

The nurse gestured to the gown. "You can change into this and cover yourself with the blanket. The doctor will be in shortly."

Holden's eyes flicked to the gown, then back to her. "I'll give you a minute."

She nodded, and he slipped out.

Eve changed slowly. The gown was thin, cool against her skin. She sat on the table, blanket across her lap, fingers twisted in a quiet knot.

Holden returned and settled into the chair across from her. His posture was calm, but his fingers tapped once against his thigh—an unconscious signal.

"You okay?" he asked softly.

She gave him a faint smile. "I don't know what to expect."

A knock. The door opened.

"Good morning," said a woman with calm eyes and an easy smile. "I'm Dr. Vega."

She shook Holden's hand, then turned to Eve. "Looks like this is your first visit?"

"Yes."

"You're a little late to start," Dr. Vega said without judgment, flipping open her chart. "But we'll get caught up. Nothing we can't handle."

She made a few notes. "Based on your last cycle, I'm estimating conception in late July. That puts you just over seventeen weeks. Estimated due date: April fifteenth."

Eve's body went still.

Across the room, Holden shifted. *Seventeen weeks. Late July.* The date hit him like static—jarring and too precise.

Dr. Vega turned toward the machine. "We'll start with an ultrasound. Lie back for me."

Eve eased onto the table as the monitor flickered to life. The lights dimmed.

A cool splash on her belly made her flinch.

"Sorry about that," Dr. Vega said, gliding the wand into place.

Static. And then—

Whoosh. Whoosh. Whoosh.

The heartbeat was loud, steady, undeniable.

"That's the heartbeat," she said softly. "Strong and steady."

Eve's chest cracked open.

This wasn't just an idea or a fear—it was real. A life, pulsing with hers.

Holden leaned in, his shoulders no longer taut, his eyes wide.

"There's the head," Dr. Vega continued. "The spine. Limbs. And here—right here—is the heart."

It fluttered on the screen, quick and luminous.

Eve blinked hard, the sting behind her eyes a warning. She didn't cry. But she could have.

"Would you like to know the gender?" Dr. Vega asked.

"No," Eve said quickly.

The doctor nodded, moving efficiently. "Vitals are good. Baby's measuring right on track. We'll confirm everything with labs, but so far, all looks well."

She handed over a starter pack of prenatal vitamins, then tucked a slim envelope into Eve's palm.

"Ultrasound photos are in here. Stop by the front desk

to schedule your next appointment. We'll see you in four weeks."

Then, with a smile that didn't feel rehearsed, she added, "Congratulations. You're doing great."

Outside, the wind curled sharply around them. Morning light broke through the fog, but Eve's shiver wasn't from the cold.

She clutched the envelope—warm from her hands now, but delicate.

Beside her, Holden stared toward the skyline, eyes unfocused, jaw set.

He wasn't withdrawn. Not exactly. But he wasn't fully with her either.

"I know your flight's early tomorrow," she said.

He nodded slowly. "Yeah. I need to pack. Catch up on a few things."

She smiled gently, giving him space. "I should head to the office."

That pulled his eyes back to her—softer now, but still guarded. "I'll call you later."

His voice was gentle. But the thread between them had stretched thin.

He leaned in, kissed her lightly.

She kissed him back, but her chest ached beneath it.

Then she turned and walked away—envelope in hand, heart tangled in what wasn't said.

At the office, the building was half-empty. Holiday schedules had thinned the halls. Phones rang infrequently, footsteps were muted.

She stopped by her father's office. He looked up, expression composed.

She told him what mattered—the appointment, the due date, that she was okay.

He listened, quiet. "I'm proud of how you're handling it," he said. "But you still represent the company. You'll need to follow policy."

It wasn't cold. Just the line he had to hold.

Then he softened. "Your mother's waiting to hear from you. She's anxious for details."

Eve nodded and left, her heels silent on the carpet.

Down the hall, Blake stood in the break room, scrolling through his phone.

They hadn't spoken in weeks—not since they'd been assigned to separate projects.

Still, she stepped in.

He looked up. "Hey."

"Hey." She tucked her hands into her pockets. "Lunch?"

His brow lifted. "Yeah. I'd like that."

"Friday after Thanksgiving. That deli off Mission?"

"You remember my order," he said, smiling.

"Pastrami."

He grinned. "See you then."

Simple. But it mattered.

She turned and headed for her office. Closed the door. Called her mother.

Her mom picked up on the first ring, voice breathless with hope. "Eve?"

"It went well," Eve said. "The baby's healthy. Due mid-April."

She could almost hear her mother's shoulders relax over the line.

But then—"There's something else. I'm considering adoption."

Silence.

"Oh," her mom said finally. "That would be hard. For both of us. But I understand why. And whatever you decide—you won't be alone."

"I needed to hear that."

"I know," her mom whispered. "And I'll be here. Whatever path you choose."

That night, after dishes were cleared and the apartment settled into its usual hush, Maddie appeared from the kitchen with two mugs of peppermint tea.

She handed Eve one and arched a brow. "Okay. Spill."

Eve blinked. "Spill what?"

Maddie grinned. "Don't play innocent. You promised details. I want the whole thing."

Eve laughed quietly. "I didn't think you'd remember."

"I've been waiting all day. How did it go? What did they say? Did you cry? Did *he* cry? Wait—start from the beginning."

The warmth in her voice wasn't tentative. It was real.

Eve pulled the envelope from her bag and laid the sonogram gently on the table.

Maddie leaned in. "That's... the baby?"

"Yeah." Eve smiled. "That's the head. The spine. You could even see the heartbeat."

She described it—the gel, the wand, the sound. The way something inside her had opened.

Maddie's eyes never left the photo.

"This makes it real," she said softly. "Not just something *happening to you*... but someone. Right there."

Neither of them moved. Their shoulders touched. The quiet between them wasn't awkward—it was reverent.

No talk of choices. No mention of the future. Just this moment.

Awe. Peace. The tiniest miracle, shared.

Later, the apartment was dim. The heater kicked on again. Lavender drifted from a candle on the windowsill.

Eve was brushing her teeth, moving slowly. Her back ached—constant now—but she didn't mind.

Her phone buzzed from the nightstand.

She wiped her hands and picked it up. Holden.

Not surprising. Just... part of the rhythm.

She answered and sank onto the bed. "Hey."

"I wanted to say goodnight," he said, voice low.

That voice wrapped around her, steadying. She thought of the way he'd looked outside Dr. Vega's office. That image hadn't left her.

"I'm glad you called."

But something in him was off—wound too tight, voice barely holding.

Then:

"It was in Charleston, wasn't it?"

His voice cracked on the last word.

She closed her eyes. "Yes."

A sharp breath, like he'd been punched.

"God..."

Silence followed. And when he finally spoke again, his voice was thinner. Barely holding.

"I have an early flight. I'll call you tomorrow. When I'm home."

A cover. She knew it.

"Okay," she said.

Then, gentler: "Goodnight, Eve."

"Goodnight."

The line clicked.

She sat in the dark, phone to her chest.

Something had shifted. Not anger. Not blame. Just... devastation.

And she didn't know if they could survive it.

It was late.

She sat alone on the couch, the sonogram strip resting in her palms—so light it almost didn't exist.

Control had once been her armor. But now it felt like sand slipping through her fingers.

And that tiny, flickering shape on the page had changed everything.

She closed her eyes and held it tight—like maybe if she held on hard enough, something in her would stay whole.

Chapter Twenty-Two

Thanksgiving was easier than Eve expected.

Her parents embraced the moment with quiet grace.

Her mom kept her hands busy in the kitchen while her
dad set the table just like always, as if nothing had
shifted. But it had.

Maddie was invited without hesitation, which softened
everything.

There was laughter, a shared bottle of sparkling cider,
and candlelight dancing across delicate holiday
glassware.

For the first time since July, Eve allowed herself to
enjoy a meal without hiding.

Later, the four of them sat around the fireplace, sipping tea. Her mom showed Maddie the holiday centerpiece she'd made from fresh eucalyptus and winter berries. Eve had always admired the way her mother decorated—elegant without excess, personal without being performative.

That night, back at the apartment, Eve sat on the edge of her bed and reached into the nightstand. Her fingers closed around the folded sonogram.

The black-and-white image stared up at her—blurry, small, undeniable.

This time, she let herself study it.

"Perhaps," she whispered, tracing the faint outline with her thumb.

The word lingered—fragile, but honest.

Could she make room for a baby?

She didn't know yet.

But for the first time, she let herself imagine it.

Friday afternoon, she met Blake for lunch.

He thought she was repaying him for stepping in all those months ago.

She'd thanked him more than once, but he never knew what she'd been thanking him for.

Over pastrami and ginger ale, Eve told him everything. The assault. Her pregnancy. The unraveling that followed. How he'd unknowingly stepped in at a moment that might've saved her.

Blake didn't flinch. He didn't shift in his seat. He just listened—fully present.

When her story ended, he exhaled slowly. "I knew something was wrong. But it wasn't my place to ask."

"I know," she said, settling into the booth. "But you were there. And I never really got to thank you. Not like this."

He looked at her—really looked at her. And she saw the moment it clicked: the panic, her retreat, the way she'd carried that day like a bruise under the skin.

"You don't owe me anything," he said, voice thick. "But I'm honored you told me. And I hate that you needed saving."

Her smile was soft. Steady. "But I did. And you were there."

He reached across the table and covered her hand with his.

"Whatever you need. Anytime," he said. "Even if it's just deli sandwiches. You've got me."

Their professional paths had split after the Ashcroft project. But this moment—this choice to let him in—built something stronger.

For the first time, Eve wasn't afraid to own her story.

By Monday, the post-holiday hush had vanished—phones rang again, heels echoed in the hallways, and inboxes overflowed.

Eve made her way to the HR office.

She'd scheduled the meeting after her last appointment. Her father advised her to do it by the book—no drama, just process.

The room smelled faintly of over-brewed coffee and vanilla air freshener.

She kept her explanation brief: she simply needed to understand the policies.

The rep reviewed the leave structure—eight weeks fully off, with an optional four remote afterward. Forms were initialed. Smiles exchanged. Done.

Later, she stepped into her father's office. He looked up from his desk, surprised.

"Because of my position," she said, "I know I'll need to inform the executive team. But... can we wait until the new year?"

He studied her. Then nodded. "Yes. Get through the holidays first."

She turned to go, but he stopped her—his voice softer now.

"Your mother told me you're leaning toward adoption," he said. "I know it's your choice. And I'll support you, whatever you decide. But I'd be lying if I said the idea of losing a grandchild doesn't... hurt."

It caught her off guard. Not from him. Not like that.

And it stayed with her.

December arrived wrapped in twinkle lights and peppermint. Union Square glowed. Skaters spun beneath the Macy's tree. Vendors sold roasted chestnuts on the corners. San Francisco leaned into the season.

And, for once, Eve leaned in with it.

She, Maddie, and Jax became a trio—dinners, late-night movies, Christmas shopping, decorating the apartment.

One night while ice skating, Jax declared himself a skating legend. Maddie dubbed him *Blades of Glory*. He spent the evening trying to impress indifferent teenagers with exaggerated spins and dramatic flails.

Afterward, they collapsed into a booth at The Foghorn—cheeks pink, fingers wrapped around steaming mugs.

"You're improving," Jax said, bumping Maddie's shoulder. "Only fell four times."

Maddie grinned. "You're lucky you're cute when you gloat."

Eve smirked. "If he talks about his triple axel again, I'm leaving."

Jax raised his hands. "No more talk of my unmatched grace."

Then, more quietly: "You two are good for each other, you know?"

Maddie looked down, her smile softening. "Yeah," she said.

Eve tilted her head. "And you're good for us."

Jax swirled his cider. "You've both been through a lot. But you're still here. Still showing up. That matters."

Maddie studied him. "You say that like you've seen how fragile things can be."

"I have," he said. Then, gently, "Don't let the hard stuff swallow you. The fact that you're still fighting? That means you've already got the edge."

Eve reached for his hand. "Thanks, Jax."

He smiled. "What else is family for?"

Family.

It wasn't just her parents anymore.

It was Maddie—loyal even when hurt. Jax—filling the hollow spaces with warmth. And it had been Holden.

But since Thanksgiving, something had changed.

They still talked—texts, occasional video calls—but something sat just under the surface. Like a conversation waiting to happen but never starting.

He wasn't cold. He wasn't gone.

But he was somewhere distant.

Like he was laying the foundation for goodbye.

Mid-December, her phone buzzed.

Holden: My family's hosting Christmas. I'd really like you to come.

She stared at the message.

An invitation. Not just into his life—but his family's.

And yet... he'd been quiet for weeks.

Eve: Are you sure? I'm showing now. I won't be able to hide it.

His reply came fast.

Holden: Then don't hide. I'll follow your lead with everything.

She didn't respond immediately.

The contradiction—his distance, this gesture—

unsettled her.

She didn't know what kind of space she'd be walking

into. Or what Holden was walking her toward.

It wasn't a yes. Not yet.

But it wasn't a no, either.

That weekend, while baking cookies, she finally told

Maddie.

"He invited me to Charleston."

Maddie arched a brow. "Wow."

"I haven't said yes."

"But you haven't said no."

"Exactly."

"So... what's stopping you?"

"I don't know what his family knows. About me. About the baby. And he's been... off. It's confusing."

Maddie scraped batter from the bowl. "But he invited you. That means something."

Eve nodded. "I want to see him."

Maddie's voice softened. "Then you already know what to do."

That night, Eve picked up her phone.

Holden answered on the second ring.

His voice was warm, but hesitant. "Hey."

"I've been thinking about Christmas," she said.

He paused. "Yeah?"

"I want to come," she said quietly.

A breathless silence. Then: "You do?"

"If the invitation still stands."

"It does," he said, voice gentler now. "I'll make sure everything's ready."

She wanted to believe that this meant something. That distance could be closed with presence.

But even as his voice soothed her, she felt it—whatever lived beneath it still held him back.

Still, she had to go.

Her next appointment came just before the trip.

Dr. Vega reviewed her chart—labs normal, vitals steady.

"You're right around twenty weeks," she said. "Everything looks really good."

During the ultrasound, Dr. Vega asked if Eve wanted to know the gender.

Eve declined again.

She didn't know why. Maybe because knowing made it harder to let go.

Dr. Vega didn't press. She handed Eve a pamphlet. "This outlines your hospital options. Time to start thinking about a birth plan. You don't have to know it all. Just what's possible."

The words landed like a quiet weight.

You're halfway there.

So far from the night that started it all—and somehow, closer than ever to something new.

Afterward, Eve lingered in the exam room, then carefully tucked the sonogram photos into her coat pocket.

A few days before Christmas, Eve stood in her room, suitcase half-packed.

Her hands hovered over a sweater she wasn't sure she'd wear.

Nerves stirred—low, steady. Not panic. Not fear.

Just the ache of stepping toward something without a map.

From the kitchen, Maddie and Jax's laughter floated through holiday music and the clatter of a pan.

The apartment felt full again. Lived in.

Her eyes drifted to the envelope from Dr. Vega's office on the desk—sealed and untouched.

Next to it, the adoption paperwork.

She picked it up. Ran her thumb along the edge.

Her father's voice echoed.

"I'll support you. But I'd be lying if I said the idea of losing a grandchild doesn't... hurt."

Since that conversation, she'd allowed herself to imagine something else.

Something she hadn't planned for.

Not letting go.

Maybe she could change.

She placed the sonogram photos on top and zipped
the suitcase shut.

The city shimmered below the fog line.

She wasn't running this time.

She was choosing to go.

And whatever waited—she'd face it.

Chapter Twenty-Three

Charleston at Christmas held a magic all its own—woven from salt and magnolia, brisk air softened by the sea.

The city didn't need snow. It shimmered anyway—white lights curling around wrought-iron fences, ribbons fluttering from grand porches, the scent of pine drifting from doorways and gates.

The airport buzzed with red sweaters, glittering gift bags, and the chaos only December could bring. But the moment Eve stepped into the Charleston air, everything went still.

It smelled of salt and magnolia—memory layered with the promise of something new.

She didn't hide anymore.

Her coat hung open. She stood taller than she had in weeks.

About five months now.

Holden was waiting at the curb.

Their eyes found each other instantly, and the world narrowed.

A flutter stirred low in her stomach.

He walked toward her—steady, sure—but something flickered behind his eyes. Awe.

She'd changed. He saw it—the curve of her belly beneath her sweater, the light in her face. Stronger. Softer.

He reached her and placed his hand gently over her stomach, a touch so reverent it made her breath catch.

His hand lingered.

"Look at you," he said, his voice quiet, pride threading through his smile.

"Hi," she breathed, her lips curving.

He kissed her—a light brush of lips that steadied her in ways words never could.

Then he took her bag, loaded it into the trunk, and opened her door. She slid into the passenger seat.

As they pulled away, instrumental music filled the space between them.

For the first time in a long time, her arrival felt like coming home.

Holden's cottage was just as she remembered—warm, anchored, safe.

Soft shadows stretched across the hardwood. Holiday cards lined the entry shelf. A single wreath hung above the fireplace. No tree.

She didn't mind. Simplicity suited him.

While she unpacked, he lit a fire. Flames flickered gold along the walls, casting the room in a soft, tranquil glow.

They ordered Thai. The food was good.

He was more present than he'd been in weeks. Not entirely unburdened—but not buried behind distance, either.

Later, changed into sweats and curled into the couch, he handed her a mug of chamomile and rested his arm along the back cushion.

"We're going to my parents' tomorrow," he said. "My mom, Ivy, Bella—they'll all be there."

Eve looked over. "All of them?"

He nodded. "And they're hoping you'll join them for their morning outing. It's a tradition."

She hesitated, her fingers tightening around the mug. Small, but noticeable.

He shifted toward her. "They won't pry," he said gently. "You only have to share what you want. Nothing more."

There was no pressure. Just sincerity.

She exhaled. "Okay."

A beat passed.

"And what about you? What are you doing while I'm out?"

His smile barely curved. "Spending time with my dad. There's something we need to do."

He didn't explain. But whatever it was—it mattered.

Outside, dusk stretched indigo across the sky. Jet lag tugged at her limbs.

Without a word, they rose and padded toward the bedroom.

The bed was a welcome sight. Her body ached for stillness.

They moved beneath the covers, curling toward each other with ease.

Her head rested on his chest. She let out a slow breath.

She wasn't hiding anymore.

Not from anyone.

His hand found her belly, resting lightly.

Then she reached for his fingers, guiding them slightly lower.

A tap. Then another.

"That's the baby," she whispered, wonder woven through every syllable.

The first time she'd felt it, she cried alone in the dark— uncertain if it was fear or something holy.

He drew in a breath.

"You can feel it?" he asked, voice hushed.

She nodded. "Started a couple of weeks ago. It's more often now. At night."

He didn't move. Just stayed there—anchored to the tiny rhythm beneath his palm—until sleep took them both.

The next morning, Eve joined Eliza, Ivy, and Bella for their annual visit to the Charleston Christmas Market.

Stalls nestled between live oaks and brick paths overflowed with handmade ornaments, candles, wreaths, and coastal art. They sipped spiced cider from paper cups and sampled candied pecans as they wandered.

Conversation came easy.

Ivy told a story about a roommate who nearly set a microwave on fire trying to make hot chocolate. Bella asked about San Francisco. Eliza led them to a stall of hand-painted coastal décor.

That's where Eve found it—a delicate picture frame, nautical in style, with a compass rose etched in one corner.

She bought it without hesitation. Wrapped in brown paper. Tucked carefully into her bag.

Later, under strings of white lights, Eliza turned to her.

"He seems lighter when you're around."

Eve blinked. "I haven't done anything special."

"You've given him something to hold onto," Eliza said. "That's more than most people ever do."

Eve didn't know how to respond. So she squeezed her hand.

That night, the house was quiet. The fire low.

Holden handed her a mug of tea and sat across from her, fingers tapping his knee.

Before she could speak, he stood and disappeared down the hall.

He returned with a box.

The same one from their video calls.

He set it on the table between them, carefully. Like it still carried weight.

Eve didn't ask. She opened the lid.

Inside—photographs, clippings, documents softened at the edges.

A headline caught her eye:

ASHCROFT TEENS INJURED IN BOATING ACCIDENT ON LAKE MARION

She read every word. Holden and Levi. Seventeen. A summer day turned tragic.

Then the photos—sun-drenched smiles, matching tattoos. A hospital room. One boy pale in bed. The other curled in the corner, arm in a sling.

Holden.

And Levi.

She looked up slowly.

"That's Levi," he said, voice rough.

She looked again. The boy in the bed. So much like Holden. Just... still.

Her chest tightened.

They sat for hours, sifting through memories. Lake summers. Shared birthdays. The wreckage left behind.

"The doctors called it a traumatic brain injury," he said. "He's never been the same."

His voice didn't waver, but she could hear the fatigue. Years of trying to explain the unexplainable.

"Treatments. Therapies. Meds. Progress that doesn't stick. He gets... stuck. Past and present blur. Some days, we understand it. Most days, we don't."

Eve didn't interrupt. She sifted slowly through the photographs. It was his story to give—not hers to take.

"They keep video logs of his sessions," he added. "It helps track the loops. The triggers."

He didn't elaborate. But something flickered in his eyes—restraint. Fear.

The silence stretched. He rubbed his jaw, gaze drifting to a photo in her hand.

He looked like he might say more.

But he didn't.

"We all kept going," he murmured. "Somehow."

Eve wanted to ask where Levi was now. What that looked like. But this wasn't a story with clean chapters. It felt unfinished—fractured.

Her eyes lingered on one image—twin tattoos, half-hidden by hospital wristbands.

Her chest pulled tight, but she said nothing.

Holden reached for the box. Carefully, deliberately, he placed each photo back inside.

She followed him down the hall and watched as he slid

it deep into the back of his closet.

Some truths didn't need to be spoken aloud.

They only needed to be carried.

She didn't know if sharing it had eased something in

him—or broken something more fragile.

But he had chosen to tell her.

And that mattered.

Chapter Twenty-Four

Eve returned to San Francisco two days after Christmas.

The city clung to the magic of the holidays. White lights still shimmered in shop windows. Evergreen garlands curled around stair railings. Fog crept in low most mornings, wrapping the hills in silver. Cinnamon and pine lingered in neighborhood cafés.

Their little tree stayed up.

She wasn't ready to let go of the glow just yet.

Thoughts of Charleston already drifted like mist—beautiful, untouchable. A glimmer she couldn't quite hold onto.

The first week of January brought strategy briefs,

back-to-back meetings, and a flood of project emails.

Her new assignment ramped up quickly—deadlines,

check-ins, momentum.

But when the office settled down, her mind wandered.

Charleston pulled at her—Holden's sisters, the

Ashcroft home, Christmas dinners lit by candlelight,

laughter echoing off hardwood floors.

His childhood bedroom had looked untouched, as if

he'd just stepped out of it. His mother had pointed to a

photo of the twins by the lake.

"That was a wonderful summer," she said, her voice

lined with distant ache.

No one had asked questions.

Whatever Holden had shared with them had given Eve something she hadn't realized she needed—space to exist without shame.

On Christmas night, they'd exchanged gifts neither of them had planned, yet somehow both had known were coming.

His was wrapped in ivory paper with delicate winter branches curling across the surface.

"You wrapped this?" she'd teased, touched.

He shrugged. "Didn't trust anyone else to do it right."

Inside was a tiny, neutral-colored romper. So small it barely filled her hands. Soft as air.

She hadn't bought anything yet. No blankets. No bibs.

This was the first.

A gentle beginning she hadn't dared make on her own.

And it undid her.

She hadn't decided yet—to keep the baby, to raise it—but each sonogram, each growing movement, and now this impossible, beautiful gift made the idea of placing the baby in someone else's arms feel heavier. Less imaginable.

Her gift had been quiet—a newly printed sonogram photo.

One perfect foot, captured in crisp black and white.

Holden had stared at it for a long time before pulling her into his arms, saying nothing.

Later, she saw it sitting on his bookshelf—placed gently between a hardcover novel and a photo of his sisters.

January moved quickly.

Decorations came down. Calendars reset. The world spun forward.

Then came her birthday.

January 9th.

She wasn't expecting anything.

Maddie insisted she take the day off.

"You've earned a little joy," she said, nudging her out of bed. "Besides, I planned the whole thing."

"What does that mean?" Eve asked, suspicious.

"Just say thank you and get dressed."

Before Eve could protest, there was a knock at the door.

Maddie peeked around the frame with a crooked grin. "It's for you."

Eve padded over, slippers soft on the floor, heart thudding.

On the doorstep sat the most beautiful bouquet she'd ever seen—cream roses, blush ranunculus, and dried eucalyptus arranged like poetry.

She signed for them, holding the card for a long moment before flipping it open.

Happy Birthday – Thinking of You,

Holden

Her breath caught.

She hadn't told him it was her birthday.

Setting the card down, a quiet suspicion bloomed at the edge of her thoughts.

"Maddie," she said, voice low. "Did you tell him?"

Maddie sipped her coffee, unbothered. "Nope. Should I have?"

Eve didn't answer.

He'd found out. And remembered.

And yet... she didn't even know his birthday.

The realization settled around her like fog—soft, disorienting.

What else don't I know?

The rest of the day played out like a love letter to her favorite things.

They started at a tucked-away bookstore with citrus-scented wood shelves and creaky floors. Maddie pulled three baby name books and dumped them in Eve's arms.

"Subtle," Eve deadpanned.

"You're welcome," Maddie said brightly.

Eve held the books, their weight heavy in a way that wasn't entirely physical.

"I'm not sure I can do it," she said softly.

Maddie's grin faded. "Do what?"

"Keep the baby." The words landed like a confession. "But the idea of handing it to someone else... that's starting to feel wrong too."

Maddie didn't push. She set the books back on the

shelf and took Eve's hand.

Eve guided it to her belly.

A pause. Then—a kick. Another.

Maddie's eyes widened. "That's... real."

"It's stronger now," Eve said, moving her own hand

over the spot.

Maddie didn't let go for a long time.

Then, clearing her throat, she pulled back with a grin.

"Okay. Enough emotional truth bombs. Let's go eat

greasy food."

On cue, Eve's stomach growled.

They both laughed.

"The Foghorn it is," Eve said.

Later, at a boutique Maddie insisted on stopping at, Eve froze at the sight of a pale green blanket, stitched with a soft wave pattern.

The baby kicked—firm, present. Undeniable.

An ache bloomed beneath her ribs.

She stepped outside without a word, the bell above the door chiming softly behind her.

Maddie followed. "You okay?"

"It's all real now," Eve murmured.

"Yeah," Maddie said. "I know."

They stood in silence as the city moved around them.

Eve turned toward her. "Are you okay?"

Maddie hesitated. "I will be. It hit me in there—everything's about to change. Not just for you."

Eve reached for her hand. "I can't do this without you."

"You'd manage."

"Not well," Eve said, bumping her shoulder gently.

Maddie laughed, and for a moment, the weight lifted.

Things had been better lately. Not perfect. Not fully healed.
But closer.

That night, her parents came over for dinner.

Maddie bought her favorite chocolate cake. Her dad brought sparkling cider. Her mom arranged flowers clipped from the backyard.

There were presents. Laughter that echoed off the tile.

Maddie's gift was a watercolor-hued sweater—soft, oversized. "You're always cold," she shrugged.

Eve pulled it on immediately. The fabric stretched gently over her belly.

The baby kicked again. Not a flutter.

Definite. Known.

Her parents gave her a wooden crate filled with treasures from their travels—fig jam, Parisian chocolate, dried mango slices from Hawaii.

She held the box longer than expected.

And for a moment, she let herself imagine a child in this space. A future filled with these people.

She didn't try to answer the question.

But it lingered.

When the apartment finally settled into stillness, Eve slipped into her room and called Holden.

He picked up on the second ring. "Hey."

There was a pause.

"How did you know?" she asked.

He let out a quiet laugh. "I have my ways."

"You're not going to tell me?"

"Nope. Magician's code."

She smiled. "Then tell me this—when's your birthday?"

A beat of hesitation.

"July twenty-sixth."

Her smile faded.

The date landed like a stone in her chest.

That night.

Her heart moved before her mind could catch up.

"I miss you," she said, voice barely above a whisper.

Then, steadier: "And I loved the flowers. They were

perfect."

His voice caught. "You deserve more days that feel like

this."

Something lingered in his words—unspoken, fragile.

Then: "We'll figure it out, Eve. Even if it's not all clear

yet."

He didn't elaborate.

Just said goodnight.

July 26th.

It would never be just a date again.

It held two truths now.

One carved in silence.

One just beginning.

Could she learn how to live with both?

Chapter Twenty-Five

The weeks after her birthday passed in a melding of motion and deliberate decision-making.

Eve threw herself into work, finding renewed purpose in the community theater project. What started as a professional assignment became something she genuinely looked forward to. She walked the stage with lighting designers, joined calls from her car, and even sat in on auditions she didn't technically need to attend. The creative energy surprised her—restorative in a way she hadn't anticipated.

What proved harder was telling the executive team.

She flashed back to the meeting.

The long conference table. The soft hum of the air

system overhead. The rhythmic clicks of laptop keys.

Her father sat two chairs away—neutral, unreadable.

Eve had practiced every word.

Her voice was steady. Professional. "I'm expecting in April," she said, eyes sweeping the room but never settling too long on any one person.

No gasps. No exchanged glances. Just composed faces—executives trained to absorb information and move on.

"My formal transition plan is ready for your review," she continued, tone even. "I've outlined onboarding support, adjusted timelines, and projected workflows for each active account. I plan to return after maternity leave and resume full responsibilities."

Still no questions. Only nods. The meeting moved on.

When it ended, she gathered her notes, careful not to let relief show too clearly. But inside, she exhaled. It was done.

As she turned to leave, her father's voice stopped her.

"You did good."

Just that.

Simple. Quiet.

But it stayed with her.

A gesture that didn't need more words to mean everything.

But the one plan she hadn't made still hovered.

Adoption.

She couldn't ignore it. Couldn't move forward without at least understanding what it might look like.

In mid-January, she made the call.

The agency's office sat quietly on a block near the marina, tucked between a flower shop and a preschool. The lobby was warm and inviting. Plush chairs lined the walls beneath framed photographs—smiling families with babies wrapped in soft blankets.

She was the only one waiting.

A woman with kind eyes introduced herself as Kara.

Eve came prepared with questions. Most were practical. Measured.

In a private office, Kara slid a pamphlet across the table. It outlined everything—open adoptions, closed adoptions, semi-open options. Pros. Cons. Legal timelines. Emotional steps.

"The father?" Kara asked gently.

Eve's chest tightened. She drew in a breath.

"It wasn't a relationship," she said. "It... wasn't something I chose."

"You don't have to go into detail," Kara replied softly. "We're here to support you."

No pity. Just understanding. And somehow, that was more comforting than Eve could have imagined.

She left with a business card in her coat pocket and a folded packet of information in her purse.

It took two full blocks before her legs felt like they belonged to her again.

She didn't call back.

Not yet.

Instead, she folded laundry.

Made pasta.

Ate dinner with Maddie.

Watched old movies.

Called her mom.

Texted Holden.

She let life unfold in small, manageable pieces.

And she didn't tell anyone where she'd been.

She and Holden talked nearly every day. Sometimes
more.

Little things—what they ate, what they were watching,
how tired they felt. It became a rhythm, familiar and
comforting in its repetition.

But even comfort has its shadows.

Some days, he took longer to answer. Other times, his voice lagged—half a beat too slow, like he wasn't fully present.

He never said anything directly, but something was shifting. An undercurrent she couldn't name, only feel. Conversations grew uneven, slightly off-balance. Like they were speaking from opposite shores, voices drifting across a widening gulf.

He still laughed at her jokes. Asked the right questions. But there were pauses now—longer than before. Silences that carried the weight of something unsaid.

She told herself it was the holidays. The distance. Stress.

But she knew.

The clues were lining up.

Whatever truth Holden was circling—whatever storm was building—he hadn't spoken it yet.

But it was coming.

One night, Eve recorded a video of her belly. The baby shifted beneath her skin like a tide pressing out, slow and rhythmic.

She sent it.

Holden called immediately.

"That's wild," he breathed, awe threading through his voice. "Alien... but beautiful."

She smiled, knowing exactly what he meant.

But not every moment sparkled.

A few nights later, Maddie broke down in the kitchen.

Tears spilled silently onto the counter. "I feel like the whole world's changing," she said. "And I'm standing still."

Eve crossed the room and wrapped her arms around her. "You're not being left behind. I need you. And this baby does too."

Maddie didn't respond. But she didn't pull away either.

Jax had become a regular fixture. More than that—he belonged.

He brought takeout without asking, refolded blankets after movie nights, coaxed laughter from Maddie when she needed it most. He didn't just fit their rhythm. He deepened it.

One afternoon, Maddie paused in the doorway of Eve's room. A few days earlier, she'd confided that something with Jax felt... off. Like he was holding back.

Eve had encouraged her to ask for what she needed.

Now, Maddie's voice was almost a whisper. "I talked to him."

Eve looked up from her laptop. "Yeah?"

"I told him I need honesty. I can handle the truth—but not being shut out."

"And?"

"He heard me," Maddie said softly. "I think we're figuring it out."

Eve nodded, her heart catching a little. That mattered more than Maddie probably realized.

But something inside Eve had started to shift.

Late one night, she opened the adoption pamphlet again. This time, she read slowly.

What kind of family do you envision?

Would you be open to contact after birth?

Are there any circumstances under which you would reconsider?

She couldn't answer them.

Not for someone else. Not with the questions they might ask. Or the ache of saying goodbye.

She folded the paper and didn't open it again.

Two days later, she invited her parents over for dinner.

Maddie helped her make lemon-roasted chicken. They set the table with cloth napkins and the fancy wine glasses they usually forgot they owned.

After clearing the plates, Eve stood.

"I've made a decision," she said, voice steady. "I'm keeping the baby."

The room went still.

Then—relief. Joy. Love.

Her mom stepped forward first, arms wrapping around her in a hug that said everything words couldn't. Her dad placed a firm hand on her shoulder—quiet and grounding.

Maddie wiped her eyes with the corner of her napkin, smiling through tears.

"I know there will be questions," Eve added. "I'll answer them when I can. But for now... this is what feels right."

Later, her mother touched her hand. "Would it be alright if we planned something small? A sprinkle? Just to make sure you have what you need."

Eve's shoulders dropped.

"Actually... I'd like that."

That night, she called Holden.

When she told him, he didn't speak right away.

Just exhaled.

Like something unnamed had been lifted from his chest.

"I didn't expect you to sound so relieved," she said softly.

"I didn't expect to feel it," he admitted. "Things are… complicated. But I kept thinking about what it would mean if you chose differently. I know it's not my decision. But hearing this—it's like something settled."

She hesitated, then said, "The truth is, I couldn't face the rejection. Or the questions. Wondering if I'd regret it. I don't know who this baby will look like… but I refuse to let that keep me afraid."

There was a pause. Then—

"You're going to be an incredible mom," he said, conviction thick in his voice.

January gave way to February. The new year found its rhythm—steady, if still uncertain.

At her follow-up with Dr. Vega, Eve crossed into her third trimester.

"Twenty-seven weeks," the doctor confirmed with a warm smile.

She handed her a paper. "Start thinking about packing for the hospital. After your next visit, we'll move to biweekly check-ins."

A fresh countdown had begun.

As Eve stepped outside into the cool February air, she rested a hand over her belly.

A soft kick fluttered beneath her palm.

She couldn't see what lay ahead.

But she was done running from it.

Chapter Twenty-Six

Eve stepped forward—releasing what had been, making room for what was coming.

Days no longer passed in neat, distinguishable pieces. Instead, they layered: appointments, emails, conversations, quiet rebalancing. She immersed herself in work. In mid-February, a new account landed on her desk—an eco-luxury rebrand from one of Whitmore's long-standing partners. She claimed it without hesitation. No one questioned her. She no longer asked for permission.

One morning, she sat at her desk, coffee gone cold, watching the city emerge through fog. Work wasn't an escape. It was a purpose. A solid place to stand.

Outside, San Francisco held winter at its edges. The air was sharp, the wind smelled of salt, and sunlight crept in slowly—as if it, too, was learning how to return. The season was changing.

So was she.

Months ago, she'd set her maternity plan—eight weeks fully off, followed by four working remotely. That plan remained. When she finally presented it to the executive team—including her father—she'd spoken without apology. There were no objections. No questions.

They didn't see a liability.

They saw a leader.

Since that meeting, Blake had entered his own new chapter—leading a full rebrand for a luxury ski resort tucked in the Rockies. His first solo account from pitch to execution. He was thriving.

Eve stopped by his office the day she found out.

She leaned against the doorframe. "I heard about the resort. Congratulations."

Blake looked up, surprised, then grinned. "Thanks. It's been... a lot. But good."

"I'm really happy for you," she said—and meant it.

He nodded. "We're both moving forward, huh?"

"In our own ways," she said softly. "In our own time."

It wasn't bittersweet. Just true.

A quiet moment passed between them—two people who had carried each other through something, now stepping into different futures.

Shortly after she told her parents she was keeping the baby, her mom invited her to lunch.

They met at a small café on Clement Street— mismatched chairs, lemon scones, tea served in chipped porcelain cups.

"I was relieved," her mom said, stirring her tea. "Not because I expected it. But because something changed in you. You didn't seem afraid anymore."

Eve picked at her scone, unsure what to say.

Her mother reached across the table, warm fingers folding around hers. "Your father's proud of you. That hasn't changed. But this... it's been hard on him. He doesn't say much, but I see it. He's trying to understand."

Eve didn't respond. But the weight of those words lodged deep.

It wasn't secrecy that had hurt them—it was the truth itself. Something had happened. And by finally naming it, she'd passed a piece of that weight to the people she loved.

She hadn't realized how heavy that might feel.

"When the baby comes," her mom added gently, "I'd like to help. However you need."

That offer settled like a lifeline. One she didn't know she'd been waiting for.

The sprinkle came and went on a soft February afternoon.

No games. No centerpieces. No unsolicited advice.

Just warmth.

Her mom curated the menu. Maddie placed eucalyptus in ceramic vases and built a playlist of soft background hums. The guest list was small. Intentional.

Gifts came in soft tones and gentle textures—a handmade blanket, a stack of board books, a sleep sack stitched with tiny moons.

That morning, a box arrived from Charleston. Eliza and Holden's sisters had sent knit hats, wooden toys, and a card: *We're so proud of you.*

At the bottom, folded in tissue paper, was a soft ivory onesie with tiny wooden buttons.

Something in her chest cracked open.

Later, she'd realize the day had marked a turning point. A gentle affirmation of the choice she'd made. A glimpse of the life she was building—held up by family, by friends, by love.

At thirty weeks, Dr. Vega confirmed everything was on track. Head down. Heartbeat strong. Growth perfect.

"Have you thought about a birth plan?" she asked.

Eve nodded. "Natural, if possible. No medication."

Dr. Vega smiled. "Give yourself grace. Sometimes plans shift."

Eve nodded. Quietly hoping the pain might mean something. That breaking open might make room for something deeper.

Before she left, Dr. Vega added, "Babies don't always wait for the perfect moment."

Eve promised she'd start preparing.

But the hospital bag remained unpacked. The tour link sat unopened in her inbox.

By early March, the apartment still carried traces of the sprinkle. Folded clothes. Half-open boxes. Stacked cards tucked between ribbons.

Each morning, she stepped around them. Brushed fingertips across folded paper. Read the notes again.

She hadn't found where anything belonged yet.

They marked a threshold.

One she hadn't crossed.

The apartment had changed, too.

Maddie was present. Supportive. But more of her belonged to Jax now—early mornings, late dinners, soft phone calls behind closed doors.

About a week after the sprinkle, the question finally came.

Eve stood by the window, glass of water in hand, sunlight slipping across the floor in muted gold.

Maddie stirred something on the stove. "Have you thought about what happens next? The apartment. The baby. How does it all fit?"

She wasn't pushing. Just being real.

Eve kept her eyes on the window. "Some days, it feels like there's too much to picture."

Maddie nodded. "Yeah. Me too."

She offered a small smile. "But we'll figure it out."

It wasn't a plan.

But it was a promise.

Since Christmas, not a night had passed without hearing Holden's voice.

But something in him had shifted.

The tension was quieter now, buried deeper—but it was there. His voice lagged behind. His laughter sometimes missed the mark. Like he was dialing in from somewhere farther away.

One night, she finally asked, "Are you okay?"

He cleared his throat. "Sorry. Didn't mean to drift off. It's... been a long week."

A pause.

Then: "Levi's been declining."

She stilled.

"We had to place him back in long-term care. It's not the first time. He's been in and out for years."

He hesitated—too long.

"He's been slipping for months. Sometimes he doesn't know where—or when—he is."

Each word scraped something raw.

She heard the unraveling in his voice—the exhaustion of loving someone through the unspeakable.

He didn't elaborate.

And she didn't ask.

They sat in the quiet. A kind of communion between griefs.

Eventually, Eve said softly, "You should rest. It sounds like... a lot."

The silence that followed was too long.

"Yeah," he finally said. His voice barely held.

Then—quiet, deliberate—

"Goodnight, Eve."

Her name lingered on his lips just a second too long.

There was no *I'll call you tomorrow.*

No *Sweet dreams.*

Just *Goodnight*—threaded with everything he couldn't say.

The call ended.

And silence wrapped around her like a shadow.

She pictured the photos in Holden's box—two boys in sunlit frames, lake water and matching tattoos.

Fragments of a story Holden had laid at her feet.

Levi wasn't alone. He was cared for.

But it was Holden's unraveling that haunted her—the way his voice cracked under the weight of memory.

It felt final.

The sorrow in him was shaped by years of silence. Of carrying more than one person should.

She knew that feeling.

Once, it had lived in her too.

She didn't know how long she sat there.

Eventually, her eyes drifted to the box near the dresser—the one meant for baby things.

She pulled it to the bed.

Inside, only the romper Holden had given her. Ivory knit. Tiny buttons.

She traced the fabric with her fingertips. It was soft. Real.

The baby kicked—sharp, rhythmic.

A reminder.

Joy didn't come easy. Not when everything began in pain. Letting herself feel it was like breathing underwater.

Possible. But unnatural.

Eventually, she slid beneath the covers. Reached for her phone.

Typed one word:

Goodnight.

She placed it face-down on the nightstand.

Turned off the light.

Darkness folded in.

The dread lingered, quiet and heavy.

But she was still here.

Still holding on.

Chapter Twenty-Seven

Early sunlight filtered into the room, pale and tentative, casting cool shadows across the windowpane. The scent of rain lingered on the breeze—new blossoms stirring somewhere below.

Eve didn't move.

Something felt off. Not loud or obvious—just the stillness that settles before everything changes. The kind of quiet that doesn't bring peace, only warning.

She lay still, listening to the hush of morning, willing the unease to pass.

It didn't.

Eventually, she shifted—slow and practiced. Her body, now familiar with the weight of growing life, moved with intention. Rolling to one side. Pushing upright.

Breathing into the ache.

Her phone sat on the nightstand, face-down.

No buzz. No sound.

But something waited.

She reached for it, screen lighting up in her palm.

One new email.

No subject.

From Holden.

Sent hours ago.

She stared at it, unmoving.

Then tapped to open.

Eve,

I've been carrying this for a while, unsure how—or if—I should share it. You never asked for the truth. And I never wanted this to be the truth.

But you deserve to know.

Not to reopen what you've tried to survive, but maybe so you can move forward.

I don't have the right words for what's in it. But I believe you should see it for yourself.

I'm sorry.

—H

The dread from the night before had followed her into morning, thick beneath her ribs.

But she opened it anyway.

The screen blinked. Then loaded—

On the left: Levi.

Not the sun-drenched boy from the photos Holden had shown her.

This version was hollow. Still.

His eyes didn't just stare—they looked through the lens. Through her.

Her breath stalled.

Holden had mentioned once that Levi's therapy sessions were recorded.

The background was muted gray. Sparse. Clinical. A streak of late afternoon sunlight cut across the wall like a sundial.

Then came a voice—warm, measured, unseen.

"Today's session is part of an ongoing attempt to sort out a recent loop. Levi, can you hear me?"

He didn't move.

Then—his eyelids fluttered.

"Yes."

The word was soft, as if drawn up from somewhere far away.

The screen shifted to split view. Wider now—his shoulders, his hands.

Fidgeting. Rubbing one thumb along the edge of his palm.

A photo appeared: Holden's family. All of them, except Levi. Taken recently.

"Do you know who these people are?"

Seconds passed.

His mouth worked to form the words.

"My family."

Another image loaded.

The hotel.

Charleston.

July.

Eve's pulse surged. Her breath caught.

"Do you remember this place?"

Levi's eyes scanned the frame.

He didn't simply look—he absorbed it. Like a ghost remembering how it died.

"Yes."

Next—Holden and Levi beside a birthday cake. Fresh candles. Recent.

"When was this taken?"

His hands twitched in his lap. Restless.

Then—a girl. Blonde hair. Bright smile. Full summer light behind her.

Levi's entire posture shifted.

His shoulders relaxed.

His eyes widened.

"Sadie."

The name split the air.

Eve's ears rang.

She could feel it again—the breath on her neck, the whisper she couldn't forget.

Then—

Her.

A photo Eve hadn't seen before. Candid. She was laughing at something off-screen. Holden must have taken it.

Levi stared.

Confused. Disturbed.

"Do you know who this is?"

He didn't answer.

Eve's spine stiffened. Her body leaned back, bracing for something she couldn't yet name.

"Sadie," he said again.

But this time, the word scraped out of him. Like saying it cracked something inside.

Eve's heart twisted. The name again. Her name, to him.

A delusion she had suffered for.

The next photo appeared.

A winding road by the waterfront. The café barely visible in the corner.

Levi shifted.

Recognition flickered—uneasy and incomplete.

"Do you remember this place?"

He blinked. Squinted.

"Our spot..."

His voice dropped. Barely audible.

"She liked jasmine. Said it smelled like summer. We met there... before I left... for the lake house."

A pause.

"She was waiting. Told me not to forget."

Then—two faces appeared side by side.

Eve.

Sadie.

"Who did you meet that night?"

Levi's eyes searched them both. Expression twisting.

He lifted a hand. A tattoo.

Eve's body jolted.

The shape that had haunted her memory came into perfect focus.

His finger landed on her.

"She smelled like jasmine."

The therapist's voice stayed calm. Grounding.

"Levi, that wasn't Sadie."

His body recoiled. His voice cracked open.

"I thought—"

The screen went black.

Eve didn't move.

A scream built inside her—raw and molten.

It tore out of her.

The phone slipped from her hand and hit the floor
with a dull thud.

Maddie burst through the door, hair tousled, panic
etched across her face.

She saw the screen.

Saw the name.

The video.

Her face went pale.

She picked up the phone, saw it had restarted, and dropped to her knees beside Eve.

"Oh my God," she breathed. "Eve..."

But Eve was gone—sobbing, body folded into itself, unreachable.

Maddie tried to pull her back.

"Eve, look at me. Just breathe."

Nothing helped.

Maddie moved around her, voice urgent but gentle.

Eve's world had narrowed to a pinhole. Arms around her knees. Shoulders shaking.

Everything inside had unraveled.

Maddie held her.

Didn't let go.

She didn't know how long had passed.

But Maddie must have called them.

The sound of the front door.

Footsteps.

A gasp.

Then—

Her mom.

Kneeling.

Arms around her.

Rocking her like a child.

"I'm here," she said. Steady. Steadfast. "I'm right here."

From the doorway—her dad.

Hands shoved into his pockets. His face drawn. Voice low.

"I asked him to look into it," he said. "I wanted to protect you. To know the truth. I didn't think…"

He faltered.

"I didn't expect this."

Eve lifted her head. Eyes swollen. Rage simmering.

"You knew?"

Her voice trembled.

"You let me carry it—like a ticking bomb?"

He opened his mouth. She didn't let him speak.

"You should've left it buried. I never asked for this."

The fury unleashed. Words she wouldn't remember.

He flinched.

Then left.

The room dimmed.

Her mom stayed.

Maddie, too.

They poured tea she wouldn't drink.

Set down fruit she wouldn't touch.

Small offerings.

But Eve didn't move.

She felt splintered in places she didn't know existed.

Everything she'd built—every ounce of strength—lay in ruins.

"I hate him," she whispered.

"I hate them all."

Her mother didn't argue. She pulled her closer.

Held the brokenness like it might lessen if it were shared.

Maddie sat nearby.

Tear-streaked.

Silent.

Outside, the city kept moving.

Inside, the scream had passed.

But the wreckage remained.

Chapter Twenty-Eight

A week had gone by since the email.

Eve hadn't set foot in the office. She told herself she was working remotely—but most days unraveled before noon. Some hours passed in a blur of emails and spreadsheets. Others dissolved completely.

The flashbacks hit without warning. One moment she was reviewing mock-ups. The next, she was back in that video—Levi's hollow eyes, the wrong name, Holden's voice breaking across the line.

She could barely focus.

Holden had known.

Not everything. Not all at once. But enough.

Looking back, she could see it now—the distance creeping in. The way his voice had started to fray long before the video arrived. He'd been carrying pieces of the truth, trying to hold them alone until he couldn't anymore.

It made her ache in a different way. One she didn't have words for.

Midweek, she sat at the dining room table with her mom, sipping lukewarm coffee as morning light drifted through the windows. They talked logistics— her due date, the half-packed hospital bag, the nursery she hadn't touched.

But under the surface, something deeper stirred.

Her mom's voice softened. "Come home. Let us help."

Eve didn't say yes.

Not right away.

Later that week, she told Maddie.

No dramatic announcement—just a quiet conversation over tea in the kitchen. She explained that with the baby so close, she might need more help than she'd admitted. Her childhood home, though imperfect, offered something she could no longer ignore.

Maddie listened. Her fingers curled around her mug.

"It's what's best right now," Eve said. "For the baby. For me."

Maddie reached across the table, closing her hand gently over Eve's.

That was all. No protest. No judgment.

They packed a few days later.

Not everything—just the essentials. Comfortable clothes. Toiletries. The sprinkle gifts were carefully reboxed and stacked by the door.

When Eve came across the soft, neutral romper Holden had given her, she paused. Her fingers brushed the fabric.

She didn't cry.

Just folded it carefully, like something sacred, and placed it at the top of the box.

From the doorway, Maddie crossed her arms. "So… this is happening?"

"It's only for now," Eve said, zipping the duffel. "I need space. And when the baby comes... I think I'll need more help than I want to admit."

Maddie nodded, but her eyes filled.

"I don't want you and Jax to feel like you have to tiptoe around me," Eve added, voice low. "You've been here for me—more than I could've asked for. But I need this."

Maddie knelt beside her, tucking a swaddle blanket into the bag. "Can I say something, and not have it come out wrong?"

Eve met her gaze. "Always."

"You've been through hell. And I know this doesn't fix anything... but maybe... talk to someone? A real someone. A therapist, maybe."

The suggestion hung between them.

Love, wrapped in concern.

Eve didn't answer.

But she didn't dismiss it either.

By nightfall, she was home again.

Her childhood home.

Spring air crept in with a chill, but the house glowed—

soft light, waiting warmth, a quiet kind of hope.

Her father carried the boxes upstairs, pausing in the

doorway of her old room.

"Do you need anything else?" he asked, careful.

Eve didn't look at him. "No. I've got it."

He hesitated, then set the box down and left.

Her mom had prepared a small nursery in quiet anticipation—a bassinet by the window, a changing table beside the dresser, a honey-glow lamp casting gentle light. Cozy. Not yet comforting.

But it was a start.

She returned to work the following week.

No slow reintegration. No soft re-entry.

Just a long list of tasks and a dwindling countdown to her due date.

Thirty-three weeks.

At her last appointment, Dr. Vega had reviewed what to expect in the final stretch—Braxton Hicks contractions, mounting pressure, disrupted sleep, kick counts.

"Stay hydrated. Eat well. Avoid unnecessary stress,"

she'd said gently. "Your body's doing more than it lets

on. We'll see each other weekly now—but be ready."

Eve didn't feel ready.

But she moved with purpose.

Each morning, she arrived early. Made lists. Sent

follow-ups. Reassigned responsibilities. Her maternity

leave plan—eight full weeks off, four part-time

remote—was in place. A line she wouldn't cross.

Work still mattered. That hadn't changed.

Her team knew the vision. They were steady. Reliable.

Still, she missed Blake.

They'd always talked about this—leading projects,

owning accounts. He was thriving now. And she was

proud of him.

But she missed the ease of knowing someone had her
back without having to ask.

Evenings were the hardest.

The time she was supposed to nest. To settle. To
welcome what was coming.

Instead, the flashbacks pressed closer. Memory lurked
at the edges of darkened rooms. Sleep fractured under
the weight of everything she hadn't said.

Being home stirred old patterns—dinner at the table,
small talk, the rhythm of shared space.

But beneath it all, tension pulsed.

She hadn't spoken to her father since the night he'd
left her room. At work, they kept things professional.
At home, they barely crossed paths. Her anger hadn't

faded—it had simply burrowed deeper, coiled and quiet.

She moved through the house like a shadow.

The weeks slipped by.

The baby moved constantly now—sharp kicks, slow rolls, stretches that made her gasp.

Sometimes, the pressure surged through her side like a silent alarm. Normal. Expected. But still jarring.

Her mom often sat beside her, folding onesies and burp cloths with tender precision. Stacking board books. Lining drawers. Not dramatic. But grounding.

It stirred something in Eve.

One night, Maddie came by to help her pack the hospital bag. They sat cross-legged on the carpet, checklist between them, lamplight warm.

Eve welcomed the distraction.

Maddie filled the quiet with baby chatter and sock rolls. Eve clung to it.

"Diapers, check. Nursing bra, check. Backup charger..."

"You think of everything," Eve said, folding a swaddle.

Maddie didn't smile. "I want you to be ready."

A pause. Then, gently—

"Have you thought about... a therapist?"

Eve's hands stilled.

Maddie set the list down. "I'm only saying it because I care."

Eve cleared her throat. Shifted.

"How are things with Jax?"

Maddie's face softened. "Good. I think it's going somewhere."

"I'm glad," Eve said. "You deserve that."

And for the first time in days, something inside her eased. Not for herself. But for her friend.

The flashbacks didn't wait for night anymore.

They surfaced in daylight—triggered by a scent, a sound, a shift in light. Her body would jolt. Her breath catch. Her mind drag her somewhere she never chose to go.

She hadn't spoken to Holden.

Neither had reached out.

It felt cleaner that way. Or maybe just broken in a way that couldn't be mended.

By late March, she was thirty-eight weeks.

Her body ached everywhere—tight ankles, aching ribs, pressure deep and constant.

That night, sleep eluded her again.

The baby rolled sharply beneath her ribs. Her eyes burned. But the tears didn't come.

She stared into the dark.

Something pulled at her.

A thought she couldn't shake.

She slipped from bed, wrapped in fleece, and padded to the nursery corner.

The box from Charleston sat where she'd left it.

Her laptop waited nearby.

She hadn't watched the video again.

Not until now.

Maybe if she saw it once more... it would settle something.

She thought of Holden.

The way he once told her to move through discomfort.

Was this what he meant?

She clicked the file.

Levi slouched in a gray room. Fingers twitching.

Tattoo exposed.

The therapist's voice was calm. Questions patient.

Photos shown.

Levi's answers came slow. Disjointed.

"Sadie..."

The name, the look, the confusion.

It didn't excuse anything.

It never would.

She wasn't looking for redemption.

But she saw it now—the fracture. The blur between past and present. A mind that couldn't keep them separate.

It helped her hold it in the light.

Not forgive it.

But understand the shape of what had broken.

She closed the laptop. Folded her arms over her belly.

A slow kick rolled beneath her palm.

Two weeks to go.

"We're going to be okay."

She let the words rise into the stillness.

Not to herself.

Not to the baby.

As if speaking them aloud might make them true.

She didn't know who she'd be when the dust finally

settled.

The veil had started to lift. And for the first time, she

didn't flinch at what might lie ahead.

Chapter Twenty-Nine

It had been a few days since Eve watched the video again.

Not to forgive. Not to forget. Not to justify.

She did it for herself—to understand.

And maybe, in a way, it helped. Not with closure—there was none. But seeing Levi, fractured and confused, trying to piece together a reality he no longer recognized, gave her clarity.

There had been no malice in his voice. No intent to hurt.

It wasn't forgivable.

But it was something she could hold.

The sharp edge of her anger had dulled—not because it had vanished, but because something else had taken its place. A feeling she couldn't name. Not pity, but something close to sorrow—for the life he was living. For the family still bearing the weight of that broken mind.

And then came the resentment. For what he'd done. For the aftermath she now lived in. For the fact that he could still exist in the world while she navigated the ruins.

She didn't stay in that thought long. Only long enough to acknowledge it before letting it pass.

The weeks at her parents' house passed in a strange rhythm—part motion, part stillness. There was always something half-finished: a drawer halfway organized, a list halfway checked, a bag halfway packed. But Eve found comfort in the in-between.

Her admiration for her mom deepened. She moved with quiet resolve—folding onesies, washing bottles, rearranging shelves with a kind of steady joy that never asked questions or offered platitudes. Just presence.

That kind of love—immediate, unconditional—tethered Eve to something she hadn't realized she needed.

One evening, on the back porch, her father found her.

She tried to pass him without stopping.

"Eve—please." His voice was soft.

She froze, eyes fixed on the yard.

"I didn't want you carrying this alone," he said, rough around the edges. "I thought if Holden could find answers first... maybe it wouldn't hurt so much."

"You took the choice from me." Her voice was low, trembling at the seams.

"I thought I was helping," he said, his voice cracking.

"You weren't." Her fist curled tight at her side.

A long pause.

Then—quietly—

"I'm sorry."

She didn't speak. Didn't look at him.

But something in her softened. Not enough to forgive. Not yet. But enough to understand.

His apology wasn't perfect.

But it was real.

They stood in silence as the porch light flickered on, moths dancing in the glow.

Now, on a quiet Saturday, the house was still.

Her mom had gone to the market. Her dad tinkered in the garage. Eve sat at the kitchen table, laptop open, finishing the last of her client handoffs.

The baby sat low in her belly now, heavy and slow-moving. A Braxton Hicks contraction pulled across her middle—tight, then gone. She rubbed her side and kept working.

Contracts. Deliverables. Transition notes.

Two weeks to go.

She wouldn't be fully ready. She knew that.

But today, she felt close enough.

That night, sleep evaded her. Again.

The flashbacks had begun to fade during the day, but at night they returned—vivid and persistent. Her body ached. Her mind hummed with static. At 2:15 a.m., she gave up trying. Slipped from bed. Padded down the stairs barefoot, spine stiff, back strained.

In the kitchen, the under-cabinet lights glowed softly. The scent of lemon cleaner lingered faintly in the air.

She moved on instinct. Opened a cabinet. Reached for a mug.

Then—

A tug.

Low.

A pop.

Then warmth—fast and sudden—spilling down her
legs.

The mug slipped from her hand and shattered in the
sink. A sharp echo in the still house.

She froze, bracing against the counter. One breath.
Then another.

It was happening.

"Mom?" she called out, her voice tight and low. "Mom!"

Footsteps. Light spilling from the hallway.

Her mom appeared, gaze scanning her face, then the
floor.

Eve met her eyes, nodded once.

Without hesitation, her mom crossed the room. "Let's get your things. I'll wake your father."

The next hour unfolded in fragments.

Bag. Shoes. Phone. ID.

She called Maddie—not a text. She needed to hear her voice.

Maddie answered, groggy at first. Jax murmured in the background.

But when she heard Eve's tone, she sat up straight.

"I'm coming."

Of course she was. Maddie always came.

The ride to the hospital blurred past. Fog clung to the streetlights. The skyline glowed in quiet pockets of light.

Her dad drove, hands clenched on the wheel. Her mom sat beside her in the back, holding her hand.

"Breathe, honey. You're doing great."

By 3:30 a.m., they reached the hospital.

Her mom jumped out before the car stopped, opened her door, helped her to her feet.

Inside, the ER hummed—nurses at stations, fluorescent lights, the occasional beep of machines.

"She's in labor," her mom said.

A call was made. Then footsteps. A man in blue scrubs arrived—badge askew, smile kind.

"Let's get you upstairs, mama," he said, guiding her into a wheelchair.

Elevator. Dim corridors. Mirrors and machines.

The world narrowed to a tunnel.

Labor and Delivery was quiet but alive—muted lighting, hushed voices, steady footsteps.

"You're thirty-eight weeks," the nurse said. "Full term. Let's get you settled."

No more waiting.

The baby was coming.

Room 634.

The door opened with a soft whoosh.

A gown lay folded on the bed—an invitation to let go of everything before this moment.

Eve changed. Climbed into bed. The sheets were warm.

A knock.

Then her mom. Maddie. Her dad.

Hands. Smiles. Unspoken prayers.

The waiting began.

By late morning, the baby's heartbeat pulsed in triplets over the monitor.

Three centimeters.

Her dad left to rest. Her mom and Maddie stayed—

rotating water cups, ice chips, and gentle

reassurances.

Just as she'd braced for another contraction, the

curtain shifted.

Holden.

He looked exhausted. Older. Like someone who had

spent nights in a storm without shelter.

Why did you come?

She didn't ask the question aloud. But it hummed in

her. Along with others she wasn't ready to speak.

Was she ready to forgive? Could she?

She didn't know.

But as his fingers wrapped around hers, she didn't let

go.

Her mom barely looked up. Just returned to her book.

Eve stared at his hand in hers. Warm. Steady.

A contraction surged.

She gripped him.

Holden didn't flinch.

He stayed.

Dr. Vega arrived after noon. "You're early, but not too early," she said.

She spoke of possibilities—jaundice, breathing support, blood sugar dips. Eve nodded.

A contraction hit hard. Her body buckled.

Holden wiped her brow. Maddie adjusted the blankets.

Five centimeters.

"I want to do this unmedicated," Eve said through clenched teeth, pain blooming across her spine.

Dr. Vega nodded. "We'll support you every step."

By late afternoon, the pain sharpened—closer, deeper.

Her mom and Maddie took shifts.

Holden never moved.

When Eve vomited, Maddie held her hair. Holden cleaned her face.

Evening brought six centimeters. Midnight brought eight.

Then—progress stalled.

The baby's heart rate dipped.

Alarms.

Dr. Vega appeared. "We may need to intervene."

"No," Eve whispered.

"We'll give it one more hour."

Time thickened.

Pain engulfed her. Her whole body trembled.

Another contraction.

She screamed.

Holden leaned close, forehead to hers.

"You've survived the impossible," he whispered. "You can do this. I'm right here. I love you."

She didn't speak.

She just pushed.

Again.

And again.

2:47 a.m. Ten centimeters.

The room shifted—gowns, gloves, lights overhead.

"You're ready," Dr. Vega said.

A final contraction built—a storm of pressure, of fire,

of release.

The pain wasn't taking anything from her.

It was giving her something.

She roared through it.

She pushed with everything she had left.

And then—

A cry.

Sharp. Piercing.

A weight on her chest—warm, slick, alive.

Tiny hands. Tiny breath.

She sobbed.

Dr. Vega leaned close.

"It's a boy."

Eve looked down, voice trembling.

"Hi," she whispered. "Hi, baby."

The pain receded.

She hadn't been broken.

She had survived.

She had held on.

And now—she was something new.

Chapter Thirty

Three weeks had passed since the birth, and the house had settled into a steady rhythm.

Not silence—never with a newborn—but a humble tranquility. The kind that wraps itself around a space when something sacred has entered it.

Outside, San Francisco's early spring pressed gently against the final edge of winter. Fog curled around the windowpanes, soft and reluctant; the air was damp, but no rain fell.

Eve sat curled into the corner of the couch, the late afternoon sun slanting through the windows in golden ribbons. The living room had become a kind of sanctuary—a cradle of presence and peace. For the first time, the ground beneath her held.

Not everything was whole. Not everything was healed.

But something was steady now. And that was enough.

She could breathe.

In the first days after her discharge, Maddie and Jax had come by. No fanfare—just quiet awe.

Eve was on the couch, baby cradled in her arms, when Maddie sat beside her, wide-eyed.

"Do you want to hold him?" Eve had asked, a smile playing at her lips.

Maddie's eyes widened. "Are you sure?"

Eve nodded. "He's calm. Just fed."

With a breath and careful hands, Maddie took the baby, holding him like a fragile miracle. She rocked gently, gaze locked on his tiny face.

"Well," Maddie whispered, grinning through her nerves, "hello, Asher. I'm your Auntie Maddie. We're going to have the best time, okay? But only if you promise not to puke on me."

They both laughed softly.

Jax stood behind the couch, hands in his pockets, watching with a softness Eve hadn't seen in him before.

He looked at Holden, then at the baby. "Guess one of us had to grow up first."

Holden smiled—wry, grateful. "Guess so."

Jax clapped his shoulder. "He's perfect, man. Congrats."

Later that week, Eve caught her mom in the nursery, rocking Asher slowly, humming the same lullaby she'd once sung to Eve in childhood. A melody carried on memory.

Her dad hovered nearby, pretending to tidy a drawer. But every time he passed the bassinet, he paused—just for a moment—to gently brush his finger along Asher's cheek.

As if to remind himself the boy was real. That he was here. That they had all made it.

Now, three weeks later, Holden's family had arrived.

Across the room, Holden cradled Asher with practiced ease, gaze steady and tender. Eliza sat beside him, gently tracing her finger down the baby's cheek, whispering something soft into his ear—things only grandmothers and newborns could understand.

Hayes leaned in, studying the newborn like he was looking back in time—like he could see his own children's eyes reflected in this tiny face.

Ivy crouched low, beaming, and offered her pinky to Asher's small hand. When he latched on, her entire face lit up.

"The most important handshake I've ever had," she whispered, eyes shimmering.

Bella, never far from a good angle, lifted her phone and began to film. Her expression behind the lens was different this time—less curated, more wonder. She cooed to the baby as she snapped photos. "I'm bringing you something from every place I visit, little man. Just you wait."

One by one, they made their own connection. Quiet. Profound. Unmistakable.

Eve watched them all—unguarded, immersed. A family now tethered to something beyond themselves.

To him.

Her own parents moved gently through the house—refilling mugs, folding blankets, straightening baby gear with unconscious care. A steady current circling the moment without disturbing it.

But her eyes kept returning to Holden.

He hadn't asked for anything.

But he hadn't left.

Three weeks earlier, in those first quiet hours at the hospital, she'd watched him staring at the baby's chest, watching it rise and fall.

The chaos had faded. The visitors were gone. The room was dim.

Just the three of them remained.

She lay in bed, the baby tucked against her chest. Holden stood nearby, eyes full of something unspoken.

"You can sit," she said, nodding toward the chair.

He pulled it close. The hush between them wasn't heavy. It was full.

Eventually, he spoke. "I'm sorry."

She let him.

"I couldn't let it go," he said, voice rough. "Not after the way you looked that day in Charleston. I had to figure it out."

His voice cracked. He blinked.

"And when I saw the truth... it crushed me. I wanted it to be anything else. I'm angry. At him."

Eve met his gaze. "You can be angry. But you didn't cause this."

He looked down.

"Sadie was his first love," he whispered. "Sometimes I think a part of him never left that summer."

She nodded. "The video gave me understanding. But I can't forgive him."

Holden's jaw tightened. "I'm not sure I can either."

She reached for his hand. "Then let's not carry it anymore."

He closed his fingers around hers.

"We can leave it here," she added.

He nodded. "Yeah. We can."

The second step came later.

A nurse had guided Holden's hands beneath the baby's body, showing him how to hold the tiny form against his chest.

At first, he looked overwhelmed.

Then awestruck.

Then—something else entirely.

Something sacred.

Eve hadn't named him right away.

She waited. Watched. Held him.

And in that fragile hour, as dawn crept across the hospital wall, she looked over at Holden—rumpled shirt, tired eyes—and spoke softly.

"Asher. Because he's blessed. Levi... because it means joined."

The name wasn't about forgiveness.

It was about truth.

Joined—not by intention, but by consequence.

Holden hadn't said a word. He kissed the baby's temple.

Then kissed her hand.

A single tear slipped down his cheek.

Now, as Eliza lifted Asher into her arms, Holden's hand

lingered on the baby's back just a moment longer

before he crossed the room and sat beside Eve.

Their eyes met.

She leaned into him.

He reached for her hand.

Together, they watched the people they loved fall in

love with the smallest soul in the room.

The future remained unwritten.

Not a clean slate.

But a beginning—born of truth.

Two families, once strangers, now forever joined.

And somewhere amidst the rage, hope, truth, and
forgiveness, Eve let herself believe—what came next
was theirs to build. Together.

Epilogue

They didn't have answers yet.

Some nights, Eve lay awake, listening to Asher's small, steady breaths, wondering how much space one heart could hold for grief and hope at the same time.

Holden felt the fracture in himself widen every time he thought of Levi—the brother he loved, the man who had unknowingly broken the woman he now couldn't imagine living without.

They didn't talk about it. Not yet. Eve kept that night locked away. Holden let the questions hover in the calm, pressing at the edges of every soft moment between them.

They were learning each other in a new way—what they looked like under the weight of no sleep, how they fought when they were tired, how quickly Asher's cry could bring them back to the same side of any argument.

But the distance was there, threaded through every lingering touch and cautious smile.

There were days when Holden's anger burned under his skin—at Levi, at the unfairness of it all. There were days when Eve pulled away, walls sliding into place with such practiced ease that it left Holden breathless.

They talked about small things. Kept their conversations safe—doctor appointments, Ashcroft plans, updates on Maddie and Jax.

When it came to the big things—family, grief, the choices still ahead—they circled, hesitant to land.

They weren't Eve and Holden anymore. At least, not the same ones who met in a bright conference room across polished wood and polite smiles.

Now they were something unfinished, raw, but real.

A family, however imperfect.

A beginning.

They didn't know what came next. But they would face it—together, uncertain, and unafraid to keep trying.

Author's Note

Thank you for reading *Unspoken– Book One*. Eve's journey was never meant to be linear, but raw, honest, and hand-won. I hope you'll stay for what comes next. Holden's voice has its own weight to carry, and I can't wait for you to meet him fully.

If this story moved you, please consider leaving a review. Just a few honest words on Amazon, Goodreads, or wherever you read can make a big difference.

- K.A. Fisher

Coming Next

Book Two: *Unbound*

Holden Ashcroft is haunted by what she didn't say. He begins to unravel the very history he was raised to protect. In his world, silence is survival. Loving her may cost him everything he thought he knew, including the one secret his family never meant to uncover.

Book Three: *Unseen*

A fractured mind. A single name whispered in the dark. In this story of memory, identity, and redemption, Levi Ashcroft steps out of the shadows and confronts what lives beneath.

Book Four: *Unbroken*

Two people. One future. A past that won't stay quiet.

In the final chapter of Eve and Holden's story, love is no longer a question; it's the battleground. Together, they must face what they couldn't before. What comes next... they face side by side.

About the Author

K.A. Fisher writes emotionally layered fiction about memory, trauma, and the ties that bind us. Her stories explore the space between what is spoken and what is left behind. *The Unraveled Series: Unspoken (Book One)* is her debut novella.

When she's not writing, she's working in education, traveling, or chasing quiet moments with her family. Connect with her online:

INSTAGRAM: @kafisherauthor

TICTOK: @kafisher.author

FACEBOOK: facebook.com/kafisher.author

Bonus Content

Curious what I was thinking while writing *Unspoken*?

Want behind-the-scenes glimpses, character insights, and secret threads from *The Unraveled Series*?

Scan the code below to request access to my **Author Folder**—a digital notebook of extras, reflections, and emotional snapshots from the world of K.A. Fisher.

It's not public. It's personal. You'll have to request access—but if you've made it this far, you belong there.